# Future Imperfect

## The Best of Wily Writers

## Volume Two

ISBN-10: 0983182426
ISBN-13: 978-0-9831824-2-9 (Wily Writers)

# DEDICATION

In 2010, the world changed both for the better and for the worse. If ever there was a year that proved to me the future is here and now, it was 2010. Yes, this future that we're living, this gorgeous imperfect future that we dreamed of when we were small has become the present.

Now, we dream of futures with new twists and turns of the imagination. One could easily say that each of the stories in this volume take place in a future where magic has returned, technology has abandoned us, aliens have invaded us, or we ourselves have evolved—or devolved.

I like to think that we wily writers are making future history with these stories.

♦

I dedicate this volume to Mark Worthen. Mark was a friend as well as a writer and celebrity editor at Wily Writers. The future looks a bit darker without him in it.

— Angel Leigh McCoy, head editor, Wily Writers

# CONTENTS

# "Loathsome Alyce"

## by Sheila Crosby

It was August in 1559, the first glorious year of Queen Bess's reign. The sun blazed. The bees droned like flies round a dead pig. Dust lay on wilting flowers.

The girl dithering on Alyce's path was like a peach not yet rotten with maggots. In a few years the gold ringlets would be replaced by lank grey. She'd be a crone soon enough. And here she was visiting one, bobbing on the doorstep like an apple on All Hallows' Eve.

Alyce sat inside, watching through the eyes of the rat in the thatch above the door. She sneered. Another customer without the courage to knock. Man-trouble by the way she chewed her lip, and unless Alyce was much mistaken, that was Ellen Woodglade, not yet married a year. If her Will was straying already, she must be a lackwit.

How Alyce despised the collection of sniveling peasants she lived off! Well, by the look of this one, if Alyce didn't open the door herself, she'd be the poorer for it.

She levered herself up out of the chair and hobbled across the room. She could magick away the pain in her bones but not restore the suppleness the years had robbed.

When she opened the door, the young woman gasped and looked ready to run. No courage here to worry about.

Alyce said, "Whatever brings you here, you'll not solve it biting your finger ends on the doorstep. Inside with you." And she jerked her head.

The girl bobbed a tiny curtsy and scuttled past, smelling of lavender. Alyce wrinkled her nose. Certainly it was Ellen. Her husband's cottage had lavender growing all around it, and Ellen's mother had a head filled with airy notions like weekly bathing and frequent laundry.

She followed the snooty cow into the house, and had the satisfaction of seeing her start at the sight of the child's skull in the centre of the ceiling, lighting the room with its glowing eyes. Perhaps she'd have preferred the stink of tallow candles. Not that she could have smelled tallow in the miasma in Alyce's hovel.

"Sit down, Ellen."

Alyce smirked to see her visitor jump. It did no harm if her visitors believed she could read their thoughts. It helped to keep them off balance. That way they were less inclined to argue her price.

Ellen looked nervously at the only chair. Would she dare to sit in it?

"Sit on the floor." Alyce took possession of the chair. The floor was filthy, and doubtless Ellen would be reluctant to sit there. Good. "Well? Out with it."

Ellen hadn't actually sat down, so she must have some backbone after all. She stood there wringing her hands for almost a minute before the words came out in a nervous rush. "You see, it's my husband. I think he has a leyman."

Alyce snorted. "Lost interest in you, has he?" She said it with a sneer, as though Alyce had hoards of men interested herself.

"N-no, but Jennet is always making sheep's eyes at him, and he still goes fishing after work each day. Only these past three days he's caught nothing but a foul mood."

"Jennet, the brewer's daughter? Her with the mousy hair and acne?" Alyce cackled. "You must be simple if you can't fight her off. Do you suck his pillicock?"

Ellen shook her head, eyes as wide as saucers. "I...I...he's never asked me to." Her blush went down below the neckline of her blouse. It was so easy to keep visitors off balance.

"So suck him! Men are simple. Praise everything he does to the skies and do anything he wants in bed. You'll have him eating out of your hand like an orphan lamb. Your mother could have told you that for free." She cackled again. "Or maybe she couldn't, given the way your father carried on. That'll be thruppence ha'penny and six new-laid eggs."

But the girl didn't reach for her purse. The blush had receded to pink spots on her cheeks and she was breathing fast, hands clenched in fists. "I have to know."

"Know what?"

"About my Will and Jennet. Whether they're ...you know."

"Making the beast with two backs, you mean?"

Ellen nodded. "I love him, but I won't share him."

Alyce snorted. "You're married, and you'll take whatever he dishes out, sweet or curdled."

"I have to know," repeated Ellen.

"Aye, I could scry that for you." Alyce nodded. "A shilling. That's on top of the thru pence, ha'penny, and the eggs, mind."

Wordlessly, Ellen took the coins from her purse and handed them over.

Alyce bit them. They were genuine, hard silver, not lead.

Ellen said, "He's fishing this minute. Will you do it now?"

Alyce shook her head. "You must do something first. Get him to cut his toenails by the light of the full moon and bring me his clippings."

"But how will I do that? What'll I tell him?"

"Tell him what you like, girl, but until you bring me his toe clippings, I can't scry him. And if you want to see through his eyes with your own, I'll need your toe clippings too. Separate from his, mind." Chances were, she'd never come back, but Alyce already had the money.

♦

Ellen must have had more gumption than Alyce supposed, because she returned the day after the full moon, and this time she knocked. But Alyce was pleased to see that she still jumped like a mouse when the door opened.

Ellen stuck out her pretty little chin and talked fast. "He's gone fishing, and Jennet's gone into the woods, picking strawberries, her father says. Her, that never does a stroke of work if she can help it." Her eyes flashed. "So I want us to do the scrying right now."

Well, well. Alyce pursed her lips. "There were six eggs too, I'm thinking."

Ellen nodded at the basket she carried. "As soon I've seen."

Payment by results, was it? Alyce jerked her head, signaling for Ellen to go in. "You've got his nail-clippings then?"

"That I have." Ellen took out a little cloth, which she spread on the floor before she sat down. Too good to share the straw with the vermin, was she? But Ellen missed the look Alyce gave her, because she was searching round in the basket again. She handed Alyce a blue wooden box. "His toe-nails be in the white cotton, mine in the grey wool."

Alyce could have told them apart anyway; even Ellen's toe clippings were clean. Alyce took a dipper and half-filled it with water. She added three of Will's toe-nails and three drops of belladonna from a black bottle, and set it by the fire. "We have to wait for it to boil."

She took a small mortar from the shelf. "So much for Will, now let's see about you." She ground two of Ellen's toenails with wild garlic and a mouse dropping. When that was reduced to mush, she added vinegar.

The water in the dipper boiled. Alyce wrapped a filthy cloth round her hand and set the dipper to cool.

Ellen watched the whole proceedings wide eyed, like a small child seeing a pig slaughtered for the first time.

Alyce thrust the mortar at her. "Drink this, then get me a nettle stalk."

Ellen took a deep breath, shut her eyes, and drank. She shuddered and put her hand over her mouth, clearly fighting nausea. Then she opened her eyes, and pushed back her shoulders. "I'll be getting that nettle." She ducked under the lintel.

Alyce was reluctantly impressed. For all her daintiness, Ellen was no lily-liver.

The door creaked, and Ellen returned, carrying the nettle with the corner of her skirt to avoid being stung.

Alyce took it from her, grasping it firmly. It stung anyway, but she forced a grin. A girl as clever as Ellen had to be cowed, and nettle stings were a small price for keeping her fearsome reputation. "Take your dress off, girl."

Ellen gasped, but obeyed. She was clean all over, with barely a blemish on her skin. Of course she covered herself with her hands as best she could, like a nun.

"Turn around."

Ellen did so, trembling.

"Mother Goddess, bless this child." Alyce whipped Ellen's shoulders with the nettle. Ellen gasped and her back jerked.

"Take her into your fold." Alyce whipped Ellen's waist. This time there was no gasp—Ellen must have been ready for it.

"Give her your sight." Alyce whipped Ellen's buttocks.

Still no gasp of pain. Alyce would have to try harder.

"Give her your power." She whipped viciously up between Ellen's legs and was rewarded with a whimper. Enough. She threw Ellen's dress at its owner.

While Ellen dressed, Alyce picked up the dipper and tested the contents with her finger. Sufficiently hot to cause pain, but not enough to do real damage. "Kneel on the floor facing me."

Ellen obeyed, biting her lip and blinking back tears.

"Now look up at the skull's eyes."

Ellen clenched her fists, but gazed upwards. Alyce dripped hot liquid into Ellen's eyes.

The girl howled, and covered her eyes. Alyce set the dipper in water to cool. "Draw the curtains, girl. We can't scry by daylight."

It was almost a minute before Ellen rose and dragged the rag across the window. When she came back, Alyce poured the liquid into her own eyes. The pupils dilated. In the gloom, Alyce could see Ellen trying not to snivel.

"Kneel here, in front of me, and put your hands in mine."

Ellen knelt, still trembling.

"By corpse's breath and eagle eye, this young girl's husband, let me spy."

The half-light in the room went out like a candle. Alyce ignored Ellen's gasp and sat comfortably in her own chair, waiting for the sight to come.

It didn't take long. She smelt cowpats, heard a mosquito hum. The riverbank rippled into view, with strong hands holding a fishing rod in the foreground.

"But I can feel as well," said Ellen, her voice high with shock.

So could Alyce. It wasn't often she got hold of a man's toenails, but she found the pillicock nestling between her thighs pleasantly familiar. Damp stones poked into her arse, and a mosquito bit her shoulder. The view changed, showing Will's strong hand swatting, then idly scratching through golden chest hair.

Alyce licked her lips in the darkness. Will was every bit as handsome as she remembered. She eyed his muscular chest and arms hungrily. It had been a very long time since a man had taken his shirt off for her, and that man had been far less handsome.

The trout plopped, but Will ignored them, evidently lost in dark thoughts. No wonder he never caught any fish.

They didn't have long to wait. Jennet strolled along the river bank, swinging a basket carelessly and her hips meaningfully. Will's gaze didn't change, but his belly tightened.

Ellen said, "There's nothing in that basket, or she wouldn't swing it so. She's no more picking strawberries than I am."

"Hush," said Alyce. "Now you've come this far, let's watch."

"Why Will, what a surprise," cooed Jennet.

Ellen snorted.

Jennet sashayed right up to Will and blew in his ear. She smelt of stale sweat. He brushed her away like a troublesome fly, but Alyce felt her/Will's pillicock stir.

Alyce heard Jennet sit, and felt her greasy head on Will's shoulder. In what she probably thought was a seductive voice, Jennet said, "Aren't you pleased to see me, Will?"

Will continued to stare at the river. "Leave me in peace. I can't fish with you here."

A hand ran up Will's chest. "Now don't be such a cross-patch with me. You know I could make you much happier than goody-goody Ellen."

Ellen muttered, "Trollop."

Will said, "How many times must I tell you? I love Ellen. Go find another man to devour."

"There's nobody else as handsome as you. Look what I could give you." Jennet undid the drawstring at the neck of her gown and pulled it wide, then let the fabric drop to the grass, revealing a thick waist and doughy skin.

Alyce felt her/Will's jaw drop. His breeches clamped hard.

Jennet stepped out of her dress and stood in front of Will, caressing a small, flabby breast. "I'll do anything you want. I'll do all the things that Ellen won't do."

Ellen said, "Why you…!"

With a growl, Will crossed the two paces to Jennet, picked her up and threw her in the river. She stood waist deep in the water, coughing, while algae clung to her hair and twitching breasts.

"You're little better than a whore, Jennet Theakston. Be off, before I go carrying tales to the priest."

Ellen laughed aloud, then started to sob. Alyce merely grunted. Evidently this would be less fun than she'd hoped.

Shrieking curses, Jennet floundered to the far bank and climbed out. "I never wanted your ugly body anyway. Your precious Ellen's welcome, I'm sure."

Will wrapped up Jennet's dress round a stone and threw it to her.

She went on shrieking. "You'll regret this. Loathsome Alyce is a particular friend of mine."

Will ignored her, packed up his fishing gear and strode away downstream.

Alyce said, "Silk is smooth and sack-cloth rough, by hanged men's eyes, I've seen enough."

The light seeping through the curtains seemed bright after the total darkness before. Ellen still hiccupped, relief giving way to triumph in her eyes.

"Well, girl, you've seen what you wanted. It's not many that get such joy from the scrying."

Ellen sprang to her feet. "Many thanks, Mistress Alyce. I must be going now. Good day to you." She dropped a curtsy and hurried off, leaving her basket behind.

Alyce emptied the dipper and saved Will's toenails, then made a fresh batch with Ellen's. While she waited for it to boil she went to the window and sucked her teeth thoughtfully. "Loathsome Alyce" was it? She still had a good supply of Jennet's toenails. The stupid chit believed they were for love potions. By morning, Jennet would have hundreds of warts on her body, the better to tempt the men with. In any case, she'd served her turn. It was clear that she would never bed Will, with or without Alyce watching.

Meanwhile she had little doubt that Ellen was looking for Will, and less doubt as to what would transpire when she found him.

The curtains were still closed when Alyce sat down again. She dribbled fresh potion into her eyes. "By corpse's breath and eagle eye, Ellen Woodglade, let me spy."

The blackness descended again. Ellen hurried along the river bank, her intimacy still throbbing from the nettles. A blackbird shrilled in alarm as she passed. She had to go clear to the mill race before she saw Will. Alyce sneered. Small chance of catching fish there. But then he was within sight of the path to the mill, so there was small chance Jennet would trouble him either.

Will's scowl turned to obvious delight. "Honey cake!"

Ellen ran into his arms. "My turtle dove."

Alyce made retching noises, then gasped in pleasure as they kissed. Will tasted of wild strawberries.

Will broke away first. "What brings you here?"

Alyce raised her eyebrows. Would Ellen be fool enough to tell him the truth?

But Ellen smiled coyly. "Do I need a reason to see my husband?" And she kissed him again. Alyce's waist thrilled to Will's strong arms.

Will broke away again, laughing. "People might see."

"So let's go where they won't." Ellen took his hand and tugged him away towards the woods. Will followed readily enough, leaving his fishing gear without a backward glance.

The lovers reached a forest glade, where Will helped Ellen lift her dress over her head.

Alyce felt the breeze on her nipples. She began to breathe faster.

Ellen rubbed her breasts against Will's chest hair while he kneaded the globes of her arse. Alyce moaned in pleasure. Ellen pulled away and tugged Will's trousers down.

Alyce licked her lips. She'd waited a very long time for this.

♦ ♦ ♦

**Sheila Crosby** lives on a small rock in the Atlantic. She's a mother, writer, gardener, belly dancer, photographer, astronomical tour guide, translator and English teacher. Consequently she rarely gets time for her hobbies, which are cooking, laundry, ironing and cleaning the house.

Her website is http://sheilacrosby.com
And there's more about the small rock at http://lapalmaisland.sheilacrosby.com.

# "Memory in the Time of Bones"

## by Nathan Crowder

Latin Boy took a step back from the window, the motion activating the soft, inset lights in the ceiling, and a cockroach scurried into the impression his shoes had left in the carpet. During the Time of Flies, bugs had been everywhere. It had been a boom season for anything that fed on decay. This cockroach was the first bug Latin Boy had seen in a long time, making it a prize catch for the small cleaning bot that patrolled around his feet in search of grit. With a predatory hum, the white dome of the bot zipped over the roach, and it was gone.

Latin Boy was good at telling time and could recite the time of day on request without hesitation. It was one of his talents. But as good as he was at measuring the hours and minutes, he was incapable of tracking days anymore. His memory was not the problem. Deep in the Time of Bones, with so few people left, Friday and Monday held no meaning.

As the cleaning bot whisked away to its hidden home in the baseboard, Latin Boy thought of the blue room. He stepped back to the window. The poor little machine, he thought, looking for meaning now that there was nothing left to clean. Someone must have told it...programmed it...to make sure the floors were spotless. Did the bot even know that no people lived in the apartment anymore? Latin boy wondered if the bot thought he was its people returning and that it would have purpose again. Maybe even now, it sat in the baseboard charging port, electrical heart burning with joy.

The thought made Latin Boy want to cry. He wanted to, but he didn't.

Latin Boy had lived not far from here once, but that was ages ago—before the Time of Bones, before the Time of Flies, before even the Time of Sickness. He had lived with a kind woman who wanted children but had never married. She asked Latin Boy to call her Mother. She was gone now. Deep in the Time of Bones there were no mothers.

When she had gone, Latin Boy had left, walking south to see if things were as bad everywhere. From Seattle to the tip of Baja, where, surrounded by a horizon of angry waves, he stopped and turned back. It was the same all over, and now back where he had started, Latin Boy found it difficult to reconcile that which had changed with that which had not. Once upon a time, this had been called the Emerald City. Now it was a necropolis. Like Los Angeles, and San Francisco, and Portland. Just like every other necropolis he had seen all the way down the Pacific coast

He looked down onto the street and watched an anemic parade of those who remained. Leather and latex, feathers and furs; signal flags of a party in progress. Latin Boy did not care for parties. But the parade had the feel of routine, of structure, and Latin Boy went to join them.

Latin Boy was careful not to disturb the piles of bone that waited outside the apartment door as he left. After the Time of Sickness, most bodies were piled outside the doors while those inside waited for what was to come. Some houses didn't have anyone to push the bodies out. Every home that lacked a shrine of bones out front concealed a haphazard shrine within.

He fell into step behind a sleek, black man who walked like a panther, dressed in cream-colored alligator leather. Behind him, three Asian girls in black, school-girl outfits joined the impromptu parade. Latin Boy dressed in slacks and a sweater, just as his mother had dressed him. He held to that routine.

Before long, they arrived at a neon-lit dance club. It occupied the corner of a blob-shaped metal building nestled in the nocturnal shadow of the Space Needle. Twin concrete monorail tracks pierced its heart. He stopped at the curb across the street. The light flickering off the tarnished, colored metal looked futuristic. Engaging in routines of the past in a building that looked like the future was too absurd for him to process. He sat on the curb and listened to the music inside, thumping away tunelessly.

A soft rain started to fall. Beads of water landed on the back of his smooth, tan hand. Latin Boy dismissed heading back to the previous apartment and considered finding a closer one.

"You want to get out of the rain?" called a voice behind him. Female, brassy, a hint of Southern California. Latin Boy turned to the row of cars in the parking lot behind him. "You don't want to get wet, do you?" shouted the voice again.

This time Latin Boy saw a girl shouting at him from the front seat of a sleek, red car which he recognized as a vintage Corvette. He approached cautiously as she leaned across the seat to unlock the door for him. The rain intensified as he slid inside.

The driver was about his age, her hair long, blonde and curled at the tips. Her eyes were the color of the ocean, and her sun-touched skin was tan but not dried out. He had seen her type before. A California Girl— she embodied playful independence and sex. "You have a name?" she purred to him, one eyebrow arched.

"Yes," Latin Boy said. He looked out his window. Through the rain blurred glass and darkness, he could see the other cars were occupied as well.

"Well?" she pushed, "What is it?"

He mumbled and turned his attention to the car interior. "Oh, I can't tell you."

California Girl leaned away from him. Her hands gripped the steering wheel with white knuckles. "Why not? Are you a criminal?"

Latin Boy made sure his hands were visible, and was careful not to make threatening gestures. "No...nothing like that. My mother made me promise not to tell anyone my name."

The short, sharp laugh of the California Girl made him jump. "I'm sorry. You don't have a mother. You know that, right?"

Latin Boy froze, his hand on the door handle. "Not anymore. Not since the Time of Sickness. No one has. All the families are gone."

The answer seemed to satisfy California Girl. She nodded and turned her attention to the neon ripple in her rain-covered windshield. For long moments, they sat there not talking. There was nothing to say, nothing to talk about. Work, family, sports, politics, religion; each removed from them one by one. The days blended together, every day like that which came before, everyone their own tribe of one, wandering a field of skeletons and perfect memories.

"Do you ever go in there?" Latin Boy asked, indicating the club with an outstretched hand.

"I don't like getting out of the car," she sighed. It was a practiced sigh. "It's not my crowd. We park and watch people go in. We like our cars and independence more than being seen. We don't need to prove that we exist."

"So this car works?" Latin Boy probed.

"New Cell energy technology, just like everything else. It will run forever unless I wreck it," California Girl said.

A slow smile spread across Latin Boy's face. He ran a hand over the leather dash. "Do you know how to get to Redmond?"

California Girl tilted her head to the side, her eyes examining the ceiling of the car, remembering. "On the eastside? I never go there. There isn't anything worth seeing. The floating bridge sank beneath the lake, but there's the long way around the north shore." she said after a moment's thought. "Did you want a ride?"

"Very much."

A sly smile spread across her thin lips. "Well, there's something I want first. Give it to me, and I'll drive you anywhere you want."

California Girl, he reminded himself, embodying independence and sex. He had never done anything like that, but he allowed her to extract whatever price she considered appropriate without complaint. Latin Boy didn't enjoy it, but doubted she cared. Afterwards he held California Girl to him in the metal and leather womb of the Corvette and listened to the rain on the roof. His hands rested in the small of her back and soaked in the warmth of her skin. For a moment, he almost allowed himself to drift off in dream. He remembered being held like this by his mother, and it soothed him.

He was lost in reverie when California Girl started the car and nosed out of the parking lot. He thought about how his mother would get sad towards the end. She would have Latin Boy hold her while she cried long into the night, his arms around her waist, her damp face in his shoulder. He thought about the house where they had lived together in Redmond. And he thought about the blue room.

They drove to Redmond in silence. California Girl's red car sliced through the still night, a vibrant ghost in a city of ghosts. Once in Redmond, Latin Boy gave directions through the deserted streets, past lawns returned to nature and others maintained by automatic mowers and sprinklers with piles of bones in the driveway. Redmond had been home. Now it was another necropolis.

California Girl did not hide her boredom of the cookie-cutter streets and houses. "Why are we out here? There's nothing happening out here."

"I used to live here," Latin Boy said. He pointed out the window. "That house with a porch swing and gingerbread trim on the corner. My mother..."

California Girl slammed on the brakes. "You don't have a mother!" she shrieked. "Will you stop saying that? You don't have a mother! You never did!"

Latin Boy ignored her outburst and clambered out of the car. He made his way across the manicured lawn. The house recognized him and opened the door when he set foot on the porch.

California Girl rolled up onto the sidewalk, as close to Latin Boy as she could get without leaving her car. "We're the same, you and me! Orphans! All of us!"

Without looking back, Latin Boy stepped over the pile of unidentifiable bones on the door mat and into the house.

He spent several minutes looking at the pictures on the wall while a cleaning bot sucked up grass and dirt from the lawn. Every photo was of his mother and him; the day she brought him home, the two of them in the garden when she was older, some birthday of hers when she was older still. All the while, Latin Boy young, perfect, never aging.

Latin Boy made his way towards the back of the house, to the blue room. He remembered holding his mother. It was nothing like holding California Girl, he told himself. His mother was soft. When he touched California Girl, her skin hid something hard, something fake. It was not her skin that was warm but what was under the skin—something that hummed and buzzed.

The back wall of the bedroom slid open a few feet and Latin Boy saw the blue room. He wondered why he had ever left. He stepped into the coffin-sized confines and sat on the hard blue bench. He leaned back and impaled his concealed neck socket upon a charged prong in the back wall. He had sat here for much of the Time of Flies. He remembered it well. His memory was excellent. It had been programmed that way.

He thought of this home's cleaning bot, looking for purpose by cleaning up his tracks of dirt and grass. It made him want to cry, but he didn't. He knew he had purpose. Latin Boy closed his eyes and remembered his mother. And he waited for her to come home.

A child of the rural southwest transplanted to Seattle, **Nathan Crowder** doesn't often write science fiction. But when he does, it gets noticed. His urban/sci-fi story "Deacon Carter's Last Dime" for Crossed Genres was selected for their best of Year One anthology, while sci-fi horror story "Frames of Reference" for Close Encounters of the Urban Kind received an honorable mention in Ellen Datlow's Best Horror of 2010.

Nathan lives within walking distance of more coffeehouses than he can shake a stick. Online he can be found at www.nathancrowder.com where he makes up words, talks writing, and stalks the great white buffalo.

# "Complete Artistic Control"

## By Bruce Boston

My implants were sizzling. I was on a roll.

Words flashed through my mind. I watched as they transposed to the screen. One sentence after another raced to completion. I had a comlink to the Muse. No doubt about it.

I was finishing the final chapter of my first novel. It may not have been the best first novel ever written, but it was *my* novel.

All at once the screen flickered and my text vanished.

The face of a man I'd never seen before replaced it. A nondescript face. I punched the reset button but the system had locked up.

"Mr. Adamski?" he said. "Lester Adamski?"

"What do you want?" I barked. "Who are you?

"My name is immaterial," the man stated. "I represent the PBI."

An official-looking emblem flashed several times in the lower right of the screen to confirm his authority. It displayed an old-fashioned fountain pen with a circle around it. A thick bar cut across the circle, bisecting the pen.

Of course I'd heard rumors about the PBI. Yet it wasn't until that moment that I began to believe they actually existed. I feigned ignorance.

"The PBI? What's the PBI?"

Immaterial's eyes rolled up to let me know he hadn't bought my ruse. "The Publishers Bureau of

Investigation," he nevertheless informed me. "I need to ask you a few questions."

"Can't this wait?"

"I'm afraid not, Mr. Adamski. This will only take a few minutes. Access to your system will be denied until you comply."

I tried the reset button again. Immaterial wasn't kidding. The PBI was not only real, it had long arms.

"All right" I sighed, "ask away."

Immaterial looked down at something he was holding. He cleared his throat before beginning. "On January 16th of last year you e-mailed a story titled 'Ripe Soup' to the *Quixotic Quarterly*."

It was a statement rather than a question, but I answered anyway. "Uh...yeah...I suppose so. I'd have to check my records."

"On December 12th of last year," Immaterial droned on in a portentous monotone, "you e-mailed virtually the same story, retitled 'Give Us Your Stale Fritters,' to *Brain Dump*. This, despite the fact that you had yet to receive a response from the *Quixotic Quarterly*. Despite the fact that both publications stated in their market reports they did not consider simultaneous submissions."

I hedged. "Yeah, well maybe, I can't remember."

"Mr. Adamski," Immaterial leaned forward, his unremarkable face looming to fill the screen, "did you really think a different title and a few words changed would mask your deception?"

"No! I wasn't trying to deceive anyone. I rewrote the story to make it better. I changed the title because I thought 'Give Us Your Stale Fritters' would be easier for readers to identify with."

"Then you admit to the facts as stated and confess to your violation of the International Publishers Code, section 37B?"

"What difference does it make? Neither magazine bought the story."

"I'm afraid that's irrelevant. If you held someone up on the street and they didn't have any credits, you'd still be guilty of a crime."

"But what was I supposed to do? I'd already queried the *Quixotic Quarterly* half a dozen times. It finally took them a year to email me a form rejection. What would you have done?"

Immaterial's expression was blank and unfeeling as a dead monitor. "I am not the party in question. My theoretical actions in a comparable situation are hardly germane." He cleared his throat again. "Once more, for the record, do you admit to the facts as heretofore stated?"

"All right, I admit to it. Big deal! I made a simultaneous submission. What are you going to do about it?"

"Since this is your first offense, the penalty is not severe. Your restriction will commence immediately and expire in sixty days."

"What do you mean 'restriction'?"

"You can consider this a slap on the wrist, Mr. Adamski. Future violations of this or any other statues of the Code could meet with more extreme retribution."

"What do you mean by *restriction*?" I shouted.

But Immaterial had already severed the connection.

The text of my novel appeared again on the screen. But by now I had lost my train of thought. I stood up and began to pace.

A sense of dread tingled up my spine, but I shrugged it off. What could they do anyway? Restrict my data access? Temporarily blacklist me at certain publications? I planned to spend the next few months working on a final draft of the novel. By then it wouldn't make any difference.

I punched up a glass of SlimStim and downed it in three swallows.

I sat before the screen and centered my thoughts. I accessed my implants, scrolled upward, and reread what I had written earlier. It was good stuff! The kind of stuff that could put me on the bestseller list.

I closed my eyes and began to write. One sentence. Two sentences. A paragraph. The Muse whispered in my inner ear. Creation bloomed within my head. I was sizzling just as I had before.

I opened my eyes, looked at the screen, and started back in horror.

The sense of dread I had shrugged off returned like a hammer blow. I was restricted all right. It no longer mattered what words raced through my consciousness. It made no difference what brilliant sentences I composed within my mind. My implants would only post one sentence to the screen. The same dozen words glowed back at me over and over again.

*I made a simultaneous submission and I will never do it again....I made a simultaneous submission and I will never do it again....I made a simultaneous submission and I will never....*

I've thought about getting a keyboard. Yet where would one find such an anachronism? I don't even know if there's a way to hook it up to my system. And besides, how could I possibly write anything one letter at a time?

◆ ◆ ◆

**Bruce Boston** is the author of 48 books and chapbooks, including the novels *The Guardener's Tale* and *Stained Glass Rain*. His poetry has received a record seven Rhysling Awards, a record six *Asimov's* Readers Awards, a record four Bram Stoker Awards for poetry collection, and the Grandmaster Award of the SFPA. His fiction has received a Pushcart Prize and the Best of Soft SF Award.

Boston's work has appeared in hundreds of publications, including Asimov's SF Magazine, Weird Tales, Strange Horizons, Realms of Fantasy, Year's Best Fantasy and Horror, and The Nebula Awards Showcase. Visit his website at www.bruceboston.com.

# "Miriam's Song"

## by Larry Lefkowitz

Until our tenth birthday, my sister and I were one person. Fraternal twins, our closeness was not hindered, but enhanced, by our difference in gender. Our thoughts were as one thought. Since we could feel what the other was thinking, we had no need to speak.

It was not until our third birthday that we spoke our first words, and then at the same time according to our mother, "Only because you had to communicate with the outside world," by which she meant the rest of the family.

When reminded by the shtetl women about our slowness in speaking—for signs of intelligence were eagerly sought in shtetl children and speaking early was one of them—she would reply, "Why should they speak? They speak to each other without speech. Even after they learned to speak, they talked with their father and me less than other children talk with their parents." It was clear that she felt apart, especially from her daughter whom it was her duty to train in the ways of the home. As for me, Miriam, my sister, my twin, was more a mother to me.

We preferred our own company to that of other children. On the infrequent occasions when we joined their games, we had their advantage. In hide-and-seek we knew where the other was hiding and would mentally warn of whoever was "it". And when one of us was "it", we never "found" the other person—that was an unspoken rule, like all our rules. The game, like everything we did, was our conspiracy against the rest of the world, against our parents, against everything that was not us.

We were the darlings and the mystery of the shtetl. Adam and Eve we were called, since we seemed each a part of the other.

While I learned Torah, Miriam, as a girl groomed for the home, was taught only a few prayers, yet she knew as much as I did, to the astonishment of everyone but us. Whatever I learned was absorbed by her simultaneously. When I was honored with a ceremony on completion of my studies, I felt that she felt she had earned it, too. The residents of the shtetl began to call us "Double Ayin" for the Hebrew verbs where the two same letters coming together are written as one letter. "Hello, Double Ayin," they would say, whether addressing me, or Miriam, or us together.

In the eyes of the shtetl our most amazing feat was our ability to suddenly start singing the same song at the same time without previous signal, even if we started in the middle instead of at the beginning, as we sometimes did. In this we were like the shofars of Reb Zalman and Reb Elya: if one was blown, the other would reverberate.

Our closeness continued, two magnets in each other's pull, until our tenth birthday. On this birthday, as on every one that had gone before, we received gifts we considered ours rather than mine, but then, at 10 o'clock in the morning—so vividly is it fixed in my memory—it happened. We were sitting in the kitchen, nibbling on the after breakfast snacks left by mother to tide us over from breakfast to lunch, when my twin began singing a song I had never heard, a song without words. Although I had never heard the melody before, it was not the melody that turned my blood to ice. She was singing *alone*, and not because I chose not to join in: *I hadn't felt the song*. I could only stare at her, numbed into a speechlessness that was the first borne of our failure to communicate, and if she was aware of my surprise (as I have no doubt that she was), she showed no sign, refusing even to send me an explanation. From that moment, we were two people instead of one.

Each day our separation increased, gradual though it was. It did not involve hostility on the part of my sister, it was simply her refusal to share—an absence, rather than a conflict—a withholding of herself that grew. In the beginning, I implored her with my thoughts, "What has happened? Why?" but she closed off her mind to me. It was as if she had died, and yet she had not died, or rather, her soul had died and her body had lived. "What happened to the Double Ayin?" people asked. "They are growing up," mother answered. "One's a boy and the other's a girl, they have different interests." She believed this explanation, and so did everyone else. People began to call us by our separate names.

Miriam would sing none of the old songs, only that wordless song which was the first she refused to share, walking to it in the slow steps of a pavan; and if I was present, to her it was as if I was not there.

Except for the song, she became silent—not only to me, which had always been so, we never needed words—but to others. Her behavior was so noticeably different that the shtetl began to contrast her conduct to mine, treating us as different instead of the same—to the praise of me and the criticism of her. But I felt no glow in their praise...I had now become one of them, and Miriam was alone. What made me despair was her refusal to be aware of my solitude: for her to have known how I felt and yet refuse reconciliation would have been painful, but that she refused to *know* how I felt left me struggling to hold on to my sanity.

In addition to her silence, Miriam began to sleep during the day, to the distraction of a mother whose imploring concerns were met with a silence on the part of her daughter, as if she had not heard her questions. At night Miriam would walk through the house, sometimes silent, sometimes singing the song, which by now was called "Miriam's song."

I would watch her in her sleep-like walk, as devoted to her as she was oblivious to my presence. When I placed myself in her path, she walked around me in her slow, dignified pavan, as if I were a chair which had been moved from its accustomed place. There came upon me the temptation to grab her, to stop her, to clamp my hand over her mouth to end the song—futile as this would have been since it seemed to emanate from her even when she was silent, as though the song had replaced that part of her that once was me. But I never did. Something restrained me, perhaps the fear of losing her for good, or of her turning on me physically—something she had never done—and which I could not live with.

If Miriam was not already the object of whispers in the shtetl, her conduct of which I am now to speak, made her so. She would leave the house at night to walk within the shtetl singing her song as she used to walk within the house, as though she refused any longer to be confined by its walls. My mother was fearful when she learned of this: What would the shtetl think? And in truth the shtetl women began to murmur "Lilith" when they saw her.

Unable to sleep, I worried. Miriam's song would enter my mind at night, when she was singing it and when she wasn't—the song seemed as much a part of me as of her, the only part of her that still was, but in an unwanted way, for I never felt myself singing it with her; she alone sang it in my mind, a song that divided us, that kept her separate from me.

In the family's desperation, the decision was made to consult the Tsadik. When he sent for her, Miriam did not resist, walking to his residence beside me as unaware of my presence as when she walked at night, her shadow more real than the figure at my side. And it was precisely this conduct which was so remarkable and frightening: Miriam did not resist our efforts to "cure" her (this was the word my mother used) but neither did she respond to them. Like wheat brushed with a stick, she yielded without yielding, remaining unchanged.

She did not resist when the Tsadik led her into his study like a submissive bride. It was forbidden to listen through the door, yet I could not refrain from doing so, a former part of me—a part I despaired of regaining— was inside. Behind the closed door silence prevailed for the half hour that passed before I heard the Tsadik's footsteps. I hurriedly retreated from the door, though it was not necessary; "Silence cannot be heard through a door," the Tsadik said to me without anger, and in the same tone, "I can do nothing; she is beyond our help, for there is something that cannot be found in any place, not even with the Tsadik, yet there is a place that there you will find it." The Tsadik's face was perplexed; Miriam's bore the same distant look as when she had entered.

Mother wept openly for twenty-four hours when I told her the words of the Tsadik, as I wept inwardly for so much longer.

It was my uncle who suggested it. Not from a willingness to help her so much as an attempt to get rid of her since, as one of the leaders of the community, he suffered from the shtetl's incessant talk of Miriam's "condition"—and implicitly, the lack of anyone's doing anything about it—more than the rest of the family. "Surely the place hinted at by the Tsadik is the Land of Israel. Perhaps the climate there will aid her," he said, as if she suffered from tuberculosis. Yet even I chose to think of Miriam's condition as an illness: it removed the volition from her separation from me. The Land of Israel was espoused by the Lovers of Zion, and though my uncle did not hide his disapproval of the youth going there, in my sister's case—for reasons of health— he was willing to make an exception.

My mother reluctantly agreed, at panic's end about her daughter. I, too, was willing to seize at any hope, any chance, to reunite my sister to me. I was given the task of taking Miriam to the Land of Israel, to one of the settlements in the Galilee where sun and work would be allowed to heal.

The settlement caused a slight improvement in Miriam, if an improvement in body, not mind. She became physically healthier—so that she worked during the day rather than slept and continued her night walks, now with the strength to do both. I, too, had benefited from coming to the Land of Israel. The pain of estrangement from my sister was not lessened, yet I was no longer kept awake by her song. I was dimly aware of it, but it remained below the surface, only occasionally troubling me with its seductive melody.

Otherwise there was no change: Miriam remained apart from me, and from the settlers, an isolation which they accepted; they were tolerant of an individual's habits so long as he or she was a good worker. If they wondered about her night wanderings and singing, they said nothing, for this was a peaceful time and there was then no hostility with the Arabs in neighboring villages to render her excursions dangerous.

It was to one of these villages to which she would walk, singing her song, as I learned from following her. Not an Arab village, but a village of Yemenite Jews near the Sea of Galilee. In the village she would stop before a certain house, no different from the houses surrounding it. She would stand gazing at it for long periods as if waiting for someone to emerge from it, but no one emerged, nor did she enter. The inhabitants sleeping inside seemed unaware of her presence, all the more so the other villagers. If they saw her on the occasions when I did not follow her—unlike my sister, I had not the strength both to work and wander—I had no knowledge. Perhaps, like the inhabitants of the shtetl, they thought her an evil spirit and remained behind locked doors when she approached. When I did not follow her, I knew it was to this same house that she went. I envied the house the attention of Miriam that had once been mine.

For I was no closer to her without whom I only half existed. My despair increased as the possibility of being reunited to her seemed ever more remote, since she continued to treat me with the same indifference she showed to other members of the settlement. Suicidal thoughts tormented me. If I could have been sure that my death would have caused her to shed even one tear—I would have taken my life. Doubting, I did not act.

During the second year that we dwelled in the Land of Israel, at the fall season of harvesting the apple crop, there occurred a slight change in Miriam. She became less remote from everyone in the settlement, except that her remoteness from me persisted. She spoke more, and her secret—for the settlers suspected that she kept some secret, and I, myself, had come to wonder if indeed she did not—seemed less burdensome. There was an expectancy about her, and a tension as if caused by her straining toward it, the effort of which pulled her partially free of her somnolence.

One night after dinner, as I lay back watching the stars, thinking, as I thought each time I looked at them, how different they were from the stars above the shtetl—the ones my sister and I used to follow, tracing the constellations with our eyes and thought and laughing our conspiratorial laugh whenever we came to the Twins—my sister approached me in her silent way. Concentrating as I was that moment on tracing the Water Carrier, I was not immediately aware of her presence. When I sensed her standing there, I jumped up, amazed at this first sign of recognition after so long a time, my heart beating so strongly I felt like a lover who first sees his beloved after an intolerable absence. I was about to reach out to her, to gather her to me, when her hand on my shoulder stopped me, so gentle her touch that I was grateful for it alone even in my sorrow at her not allowing me more. But it was her expression, the same a fawn has when it is listening for something, that prevented me from attempting to bridge a gap greater than separated me from the stars I had been gazing at. And then I, too, heard he song. It did not come from Miriam, but from a flute somewhere out in the darkness, distant, the sound growing louder as its source approached.

Miriam turned to face it as if expecting it, looked back at me for an instant—the fawn changed to Lot's wife caught in the moment of her forbidden look back at Sodom—then her face became submissive again and she moved in her silent pavan toward the sound. The figure playing it appeared, his face dark, his features not recognizable in the moonless night. He stopped as she approached him, turned, still playing, the two shadows merging into one glided down the path toward the village. I took a step toward them, toward my twin who was not my twin, but a slight movement of her finger, discernable from his only by its slimness that I knew better than my own finger, made without her turning her head or even slowing her step, stopped me. I knew she would not hesitate this time outside the house in the village. I knew, too, as I felt the song being pulled out of me forever, that in fusing her soul with another's, she had freed my own.

The stories, poetry, and humor of **Larry Lefkowitz** have appeared in many publications in the U.S., Israel, and Britain. Among them: *A Cappella Zoo, Third Wednesday Magazine, The Vocabula Review, The Literary Review, Midstream*, e-zines, anthologies. Lefkowitz is looking for a publisher for his novel "Lieberman." The plot of the novel concerns a literary critic, the assistant to the literary critic, and the wife of the critic. Very literary and filled with humor. Excerpts and chapters have been published in print and online.

# "9 Curzon Place"

## by Daniel W. Powell

The man at the center of the circle looked haggard—wasted by excess. He wore skin-tight jeans and a dingy t-shirt stained with vomit. His oily hair sprang from his scalp in jagged angles and tears brimmed his swollen eyes before tracking down gaunt cheeks.

He was fielding questions near the entrance to the flat where it happened.

"Describe the kind of person Caleb Perrilloux was," a reporter said, shoving her microphone into the man's face. Flashbulbs crackled all around them. A mournful wailing, the sound of distraught fans on the periphery of the media throng, provided an eerie soundtrack to the proceedings.

"He was just the best. The best friend. The best musician. The best...I...I can't say anything other than that," the man gasped in response.

The reporters clamored to deliver the next question until one of them was able to shout above the rest. "Who found him, Mr. Strong?"

Sammy Strong, the drummer for the mega-band Perrilloux, wiped his eyes. "It was our road manager. Beth Howser. She'd only just re-joined the tour after seeing to some personal business back in the states."

Another crush of questions, then, "Were drugs involved in Caleb's death?"

Strong narrowed his eyes at the reporter before he sprang at him, trying to collar the unassuming man in the trench coat. Members of the band's entourage held him back and Strong, tears now streaming from his eyes, shouted at him. "Fuck you, man! Caleb never did drugs! Never! I don't want any mistakes about that. The rest of us are fuck-ups, man, but Caleb never did that shit!"

"Ok, ok. That's it for now, folks. We'll answer more of your questions after the autopsy." This was Howser. The media horde parted as a limousine pulled up to the curb and she and the three remaining band members ducked into the car. She spared the building a single glance as they pulled into the street and watched as 9 Curzon Place faded in the distance.

*i*

He sat, bookended by a pair of leggy groupies, in the rear of the bus and marveled at his band mates' ability to get trashed on such a short ride. Of course, he knew that Sammy had taken the stage in a state of advanced pollution. Probably Billy as well—he was using a lot more these days.

But less than three miles? By the sounds of their celebration, they understood on some level that the show had been amazing. For that, Caleb Perrilloux remained thankful. At least they could still appreciate the energy of a great performance.

The problem was with the prescription pad. OxyContin. Vicodin. Percocet. Valium. The news of Heath Ledger's death hadn't even made a dent in their abuse. If anything, Sammy had upped the ante. And that wasn't to say that his band mates didn't appreciate the traditional vices, either. Sammy *always* had blow on him and Billy and Mike smoked a couple of joints every day. And then there were those little green bottles—the ubiquitous scads of Heineken. Caleb didn't know where they came from or how they got there, but every hotel room, every dressing room, ever airplane or charter bus or limousine they rode in was filthy with them.

Caleb fingered silent chords on the Fender in his lap while one of the groupies—a brunette with augmented breasts, a French manicure and absolutely no underwear—sidled up to him and nibbled on his ear lobe. The blonde on his left was spaced out on something heavy. Her head flopped back and forth from Caleb's shoulder to the seat cushion and she slowly blinked her eyes as the driver navigated the warren of streets from the Palladium House to their new lodgings.

For about the thirtieth time in the last forty-eight hours, Caleb longed for Beth. He'd come to realize just how much they relied on her in the last week, since she'd been called back to Maryland to tend to her stricken father.

Caleb checked his watch. If she made her flight in D.C., Beth was probably just approaching London airspace. She'd meet them in an hour and Caleb would take her out to dinner to discuss the shows.

And to get away from the rest of them.

He considered them as the bus surged through the streets. He loved them. They were his family, and that's why it made it all the more difficult to watch them consume themselves. Sam and Mike he'd known since grade school. Billy joined the band in high school. All of them had cut their teeth in the swamplands of Northern Louisiana. It was where they'd fused bluegrass with southern rock. The resulting sound was a thing to behold and Perrilloux had taken the country by storm. Their debut scorched up the charts and sold eight million copies worldwide. The follow-up had been even better regarded and they were on their way. Their first European tour had gone fairly well, up until Sammy had blacked the eye of a porter at The Essex House before trashing his suite. They'd been bounced and Beth hadn't been there to book the replacement lodging. Dizzy Callahan, their production manager back in Dallas, had found this new place sight unseen from the comforts of his penthouse office.

As he watched Sammy make out with an under-aged groupie up front, Caleb endured a moment of acute anxiety. Something was off. He pushed the brunette away and disappeared into the bathroom.

He rinsed his face with cold water and studied himself. He looked ok. A little tired, maybe, but none the worse for wear. He avoided the drugs and alcohol like they were irradiated. He'd tried them—only to become horrified when they dulled his sense of musicianship. They separated him from the thing that made him happiest—the music—and that would have been a loss to the world.

Because Caleb Perrilloux was just about the second coming of Jimi Hendrix. From the time he could hoist a six-string, he'd been a guitar virtuoso. Critics loved him. Musicians envied him. His fans adored him.

And in turn, he committed himself to his craft. He worked at it for hours every day. He could do things with an axe that 99% of the world's finest could only dream of, and he did it night after night. The magazines gushed about his phrasing. The critics raved about his fingering. The documentary of their U.S. tour portrayed his work ethic in glowing terms, and the public loved his demeanor.

Caleb Perrilloux was the opposite of the typical rock star. He was engaging and bright with the media. He signed autographs and made time for fans. He offered opinions on world events and politics and he hadn't lost the "aw-shucks" veneer that had come to personify him through the years because he *couldn't*. It was really him. Despite the band's success, he was still the guitar phenom from Baton Rouge that had been raised to respect others and enjoy the fruits of a life well lived.

He exited the bathroom, stashed his guitar and took a seat by himself at the window. The bus trundled through the streets, bullying smaller vehicles out of the way. Caleb noted the street signs as they inched their way through London. Regent. Conduit. Bruton. Berkeley. When they turned onto Curzon Street, that signal flare in his belly went off again.

The bus lurched to a stop in front of a three-story stone building. It was bordered by a high, wrought iron fence and had white trim around the windows. "Everybody off! These are the new digs!" Chief called. Chief Jones was the head roadie. He handled the driving duties and sound checks. "Ya'll have flats ten, eleven and twelve at your disposal. No repeats of last night's shenanigans!"

Sammy and Mike and Billy whooped it up as they herded their groupies down the aisle and into the streets where, despite the hour approaching midnight, the sidewalks were packed. Caleb grabbed his guitar and climbed down. He scanned up the street to where a place called the Playboy Club was teeming with scantily clad young women and men in fancy suits.

The band was enveloped by fans and Caleb chatted for twenty minutes before taking his leave. Chief waited him out on the staircase. He held the door for him and, despite the feeling that he was walking into one of those dark swamps outside of Baton Rouge—the kind with only one way in and one way out—Caleb followed him into the building.

"Dizzy booked the top three flats for you guys. I'm going to sleep in the bus. Make sure we don't get any overzealous fans in there with your things. You guys had a great show tonight, Caleb. Just a great show. Don't celebrate too hard." He clapped the young man on the shoulder and laughed at his little joke. Chief knew that Caleb was more apt to spend the night playing his guitar than hanging with the rest of them.

"So long, Chief," Caleb called as the roadie descended the steps.

Jones turned. "Hey, now! Don't say it like that! I'll see you in the morning, kid."

Caleb nodded and began to climb the stairs to the third floor.

*ii*

The picture was only two months old. It sat on an easel to the left of the table where the surviving members of Perrilloux were fielding questions about their friend's death.

The enlarged photograph showed a young, thin man standing in a doorway, bracing himself with his arms above his head. He had a full head of shaggy brown hair, intelligent brown eyes and full red lips. His guitar was slung over his shoulders and he wore a sweater and blue jeans in the cool air of Berlin, where the photograph had been taken.

He was twenty-three years old.

"And what did the autopsy reveal, Ms. Howser?"

"Caleb Perrilloux drowned," Beth replied, surprised at the even tone of her voice. "Investigators found a large quantity of water in his lungs. The investigation into who was with him on the night of his death is ongoing."

"Didn't you discover his body, Ms. Howser?"

"I did. I'd just arrived at the flat after business in the United States. I had to have the door…forced open when I sensed something was wrong."

"And how did you come to sense that, Ms. Howser?"

"The carpet in the hallway was damp. That and…well, I just had a feeling that something was wrong in there."

"Are you aware of the history of that flat, Ms. Howser?"

Beth Howser bit her lip as she considered her response.

### iii

Billy had a groupie's top off when Caleb entered the flat. He was drizzling champagne onto her breasts and licking it off of her erect nipples. Sammy and Mike were attending to their own paramours. Groups of random men and women from the club up the street milled about the flat, drinks in hand. Loud music—Radiohead—blasted from the sound system in the front room. Someone had put the replay of a muted soccer match on the big screen television in the den and a group of men cheered as a player was cut down in the penalty box. There would be a free kick.

Caleb drifted from room to room. Women gravitated to him like bees to pollen but he politely rebuked them until he found a quiet bedroom down a long hallway in the rear of the flat. He slipped into the room, sat and massaged his temples. He checked his watch again. Beth would be collecting her bags and waiting on the driver she'd arranged prior to leaving D.C.

The throbbing bass line bled through the walls but he couldn't hear it anymore. He pulled the guitar from its case and began working through the chords, whipping his fingers up and down the fret board. After thirty minutes he was on fire and all alone in his world, so it took three separate bouts of knocking at the door to finally wrest his attention. He expected Beth. What he got was one of the Playboy bunnies from the club across the street. Red garters held up a pair of fishnet stockings. She wore a pair of fuzzy bunny ears and a matching red bra. She'd lost her panties somewhere in the flat.

"Hi, Caleb. Can I keep you company?"

He felt deflated. Where was Beth? All he wanted was to spend the night speaking with her. He was worried about her father. Worried about his band mates.

"No," he replied evenly. "No. I don't need your company. In fact, I'd like to have this place to myself."

She looked confused. It was clear she wasn't used to being dismissed. Caleb put his guitar down and motioned her down the hallway. He marched over to the stereo and turned off the music, drawing the requisite protest from the crowd. "Listen, everybody! Thanks for your support and for making London such an amazing place to play rock and roll," they began to hoot and holler, "but you'll need to take the party down the way. Everybody out. We have flats ten and eleven on the other side of the building. Ya'll don't have to go home, but you can't stay here!" He called. This drew a good-natured laugh from the crowd and Sammy stood on the coffee table, a Heineken held high.

"To Caleb!" he slurred, and the crowd cheered. "Our best friend. Our best *influence*…and our best musician!" The crowd offered another cheer and Caleb felt a flush of warmth as they made their way down the hall, congratulating him on the London shows and the success of the band.

Mike hung back a moment and when it was just the two of them in Flat 12, a sly smile formed on his face. "You going to make a move on Beth tonight, aren't you?"

Caleb flushed again. He shrugged. "I'm excited to see her."

Mike burst out laughing and clapped him on the back. "She's a good girl, brother. What are you going to do in the meantime? You want some company?"

Caleb was touched by the offer. "You go ahead. I'm working on a few things for a new song I'm writing. Have some fun, Mike, and I'll see you for some breakfast in the morning."

The bassist considered his friend. "Ok, Caleb. But all work and no play…"

"I know, I know," Caleb insisted. He threw his arm around Mike's shoulders and walked him to the doorway. "Don't trash the place. I get the feeling the tab would be a bit steep around these parts."

Mike smiled and nodded and then was gone down the hallway. Caleb closed the door. He was alone in Flat 12, at 9 Curzon Place. As he walked back to his bedroom, he thought he heard a sigh in the sudden silence of the place.

*iv*

"It's a bit of a mystery," the lead investigator, a bear of a man named Mullins, admitted. "There was no sign of struggle. No drugs in his system. No sign of forced entry. No tampering with the windows."

"And so you're still operating on the theory of suicide?" a reporter asked.

"It's all we have. But the deceased showed no typical signs of depression. And to end a life in that fashion—it's just a very hard thing to accomplish. Even when the person loses consciousness, the body attempts to preserve itself. It's almost impossible to drown oneself without the aid of drugs."

"Have you considered the paranormal?" one reporter asked. "There are those who are trained to investigate situations like these."

The big man sneered. "How do you mean, 'situations like these'?"

The woman, a thin Brit who wore her hair in a bun, replied, "Situations with no clear resolution."

*v*

He labored over his guitar, a legal pad covered in scrawled lyrics on the bed next to him. He worked through chord progressions and practiced the same tricky sequence time and time again.

*I'm a stranger...in a strange land*, he sang *in a world that needs me gone*

He had worked up a light sweat and more than an hour had passed when things suddenly crystallized and he became aware of the time. It was almost two. He had the unmistakable feeling that something very bad had happened to Beth.

He tried her on his cell phone but the call wouldn't go through. He listened to the recording. In a severe British accent, a woman stated: *The hour is very late in London and our services are currently out of order. If you have an emergency, please hang up the phone and contact the field agent for your territory. Thank you. The hour is very late in London…*

Funny how they chose to word things over here, he thought. He hung up the phone and slipped down the hallway and into the master bathroom. There was an ornate stained glass bathtub decorated with trees and shrubs. Opposite the tubs was a pair of mirrors. One was in the shape of an apple tree, the other an oval looking glass.

Caleb closed his eyes and splashed water over his face. When he opened them, the mirror reflected a hangman's noose over his left shoulder. He made a frightened little noise and wheeled to see how it got there, but the space was empty.

He rubbed his eyes, ran his fingers through his hair. "Jesus," he whispered, "you're supposed to be the sober one, Caleb."

He turned back to the mirror, thankful that the noose hadn't reappeared.

He was brushing his teeth when the opening riffs of "Who Are You" began to thunder through the sound system. Caleb rinsed his mouth and strode down the hallway to the den, where the little lights on the stereo equalizer were jumping in time with Keith Moon's obsessive drumming.

"All right, who put the music on?" he called. "Sammy? Is this you? I told you, I wanted to get some rest tonight…"

He adjusted the sound to a conversational volume and could just make out a trickle of laughter coming from down the hallway. Warily, he headed for the kitchen. He pushed open the swinging door, his eyes scanning the huge galley. In the corner, an enormous woman sat at a prep table. Her back was to him. She was hunched over a plate of food. She was going at her meal with a vengeance, that discordant giggling coming from her as she chewed her food.

"Look, I don't who you are or who let you in here, but you'll have to leave," he said, starting toward her earnestly.

She turned to peer over her shoulder and loosed a deep bellow of anguish, mouth wide and filled with partially chewed food. Her rotten teeth were sharp. Caleb sprang back, startled by her reaction. His legs knocked together and he stumbled a few steps in fear before bracing himself on a counter.

She wore her black hair in a beehive. Her sallow skin collected in a billowy pocket beneath her chin, and her glossy eyes appeared...well, dead.

The music in the living room changed, the instantly recognizable opening stanza of The Mamas & the Papas' "California Dreamin'" surging through the speakers that had been wired into each of the rooms. Caleb suddenly recognized her.

It was Cass Elliot. Mama Cass.

She snatched up the plate and showed him her meal. Caleb put a hand to his mouth to keep from being sick. It was a ham sandwich. It teemed with maggots. A sly smile formed on her lips and she raised the plate and ate from it like a dog, starting in with the giggling again.

Caleb turned and exited the kitchen. He was overcome with nausea. He fell to the floor and vomited in the hallway. He had to get out of there. The air felt…poisoned.

Where was Beth?

The music changed again, growing still louder. The Who's "Won't Get Fooled Again" pulsed through the walls.

Caleb crawled down the hallway. The door to the kitchen swung open behind him and Cass Elliot, still giggling, watched his progress with tiny dark eyes buried in folds of skin. Caleb spared her a glance, spotted a glistening piece of ham in the corner of her slightly parted lips and vomited again.

"In here," someone called. "Hurry! She'll leave you alone if you can make it!" The voice was coming from one of the spare bedrooms. Caleb crawled to it and when he crossed the threshold, he instantly felt better.

Until he looked up and saw Keith Moon reclining in an easy chair. Moon stuck a pill in his mouth, chewed it and chased it with a swig of champagne. The television in the corner flickered once, twice. A picture flashed there. There was no sound. A zombie lurched across the screen to plant a kiss on a fetching actress.

"It's *The Abominable Dr. Phibes*. I love it. Can't ever get enough of it. It's scary and funny all at once. You want one?" He showed Caleb his hand, which was filled with little white pills.

Caleb shook his head.

"I see. Sober, are you? Well, you sure picked a hell of a place to spend the night, kid. Hell of a place." He popped another pill and started laughing as the zombie on the screen shrugged into a smoking jacket.

"What…" Caleb croaked.

Moon popped another pill. "It'll only be a few hours till it's light out, kid. You'd better get started.

This place...it doesn't mess around. Just give it what it wants and you'll become one of us."

A hammering set of knocks came at the door. It shuddered in its frame. "Let us be, Cass! We're taking care of business in here!"

"How..." Caleb said. He pushed himself into a sitting position and leaned against the wall. Every movement threatened another wave of excruciating nausea.

Moon laughed. "The rock gods, man! Where do you think all those great songs come from, huh? You didn't think they'd let us have them for free did you?"

"I don't," Caleb's voice was a whisper, "get it. Rock gods?"

He became aware of a low murmur. It came from the bathroom. He could hear the sound of rushing water.

Moon laughed again at the television, then he fixed Caleb with a shrewd glare. There was menace in it. "I don't know how you found this place, but it has a very bad vibe, son. It pulls us in, like one of those plants that eats insects. You're here with the rest of us," he motioned with his hand, "and your future's on the other side of that door."

Caleb followed his finger to the bathroom door. The knob slowly rotated and the door inched open. Water was just beginning to crest the rim of the claw-foot bathtub and fall in a wet curtain onto the linoleum.

The murmuring grew louder. It took on a new dimension, a harmony and pacing that suddenly seemed lyrical to him. It was actually quite beautiful.

Moon popped a pill, swallowed champagne. "Oh, yeah! You're hearing it now, aren't you kid? They make some kind of sound, those ancient ones. Before too long, we'll have a great band in here. Cass ain't much on the eyes, but she's got a set of pipes on her. I can handle the drumming. You take care of the guitar. Yes sir, pretty soon we'll have a hell of a band…"

Caleb used the wall to brace himself as he climbed to his feet. There was something in that room pulling him…drawing him forward. He stumbled toward the rhythmic chanting. He spared a glance over his shoulder, where moon was laughing at the movie. After a moment he locked eyes with the younger man. His face became very sad.

"It's just the balance of things, kid. Just the balance of things." He turned back to the television with a laugh and popped another pill.

Caleb entered the bathroom. The room was filled with steam. Above the bathtub he could see a shimmering disturbance, an invisible cloud that was nevertheless…*palpable*, somehow. It seemed the chanting was coming from the cloud, and when he climbed into the warmth of the bath, a dozen hands pulled him down and held him fast to the bottom.

He watched the world shimmering above him through eighteen inches of clear water. Then things became hazy and he was enveloped in a cloud of light and the world was filled with a rhythmic chanting that was older than man.

*vi*

Beth Howser wouldn't go into Flat 12 at 9 Curzon Place unless it was the middle of the day. The rest of the band had returned to Louisiana. She couldn't bring herself to go with them, though. She had rented a place in London, feeling closer to the man she had just begun to love. She thought Caleb had been developing an interest in her as well.

On a gray afternoon in mid-April, she entered the flat at just after one p.m. Alyssa Crowley accompanied her. Crowley carried a Sony micro-recorder that could pick up the faintest of sounds.

Crowley charged her clients 100 pounds per hour to speak with the dead.

They began in the den and worked their way toward the kitchen.

"There are so many here," Crowley said. She lightly moved her hands over the furnishings, over the countertops. She closed her eyes, the lids trembling as she navigated the rooms by sense of touch. "So many that have passed here before. This is a place of great power. Caleb is a part of it."

Beth's breath caught in her chest at the sound of his name. "Can you sense him right now?"

"Not in this room. But he's close."

They moved back into the hallway, past the den and toward the bathroom where they said he had taken his life. Beth still didn't believe it had been suicide.

Crowley took two steps toward the bathroom, then was leveled by an unseen force. It was like she'd been hit by a half back in a rugby match. She offered one clipped shriek of surprise and then was on her back on the floor, eyes rolled up in her sockets. She clenched and unclenched her fists at her sides and began to speak.

"We can collect you now, Beth," she spat in a guttural tongue. Her voice had dropped a couple of registers. "He is here with us…"

Beth sank to Crowley's side. "Caleb? Can you hear me? What happened to you, Caleb?"

"You will make him happy. Return this night…" the door to the bathroom where she had found him slammed shut, opened again and slammed shut. "Join us!"

"No. Let him rest. Let him have peace!" she cried.

"You will give him rest…"

Beth grabbed Crowley beneath her armpits. She began to drag her through the room and back down the hall. When she arrived at the front door, she let Crowley slip to the floor and opened it. A figure blurred by in the corner of her peripheral vision. Whatever it was, it was large and fast. She heard a strange giggling coming down the hallway. She hoisted the medium again, drug her into the hallway and the door snapped shut behind her. There was a sound like a sigh, and then Crowley came to.

"What happened? How long have I been out?"

"Maybe ten minutes," Beth replied. "Come on. We need to get out of this building. It's not safe."

They hurried down the steps and out into the gray afternoon light and Beth took a final look at 9 Curzon Place before devoting her attention to hailing a cab.

*vii*

They sat in a dim little café, tucked into the corner with steaming cups of tea.

"Do you care to listen to it?" Crowley asked.

Beth bit her lip and nodded. Crowley reached out and squeezed her hand for comfort. She turned on the recorder. The first eight minutes were filled with crackling hisses and pops, then there was Crowley snarling in that strange voice.

Beth wondered if she was even the littlest bit embarrassed by it, but Crowley only appeared deeply concerned. She sipped her tea with hands that didn't shake.

The recording terminated and Crowley regarded her American client with apprehension. "I'm sorry there's nothing more conclusive here, dear."

But Beth thought there was. She looked hopeful for the first time in days. "Rewind that last part. I think I heard something. Turn it up."

Crowley did and, sure enough, there he was. It was unmistakably his voice, that yowling lowland moxie that had endeared him to so many over the years.

*I'm a stranger...in a strange land,*
*In a world that needs me gone.*

They sat in the café sipping tea and listening to Caleb Perrilloux's final recording, that haunting final discourse of 9 Curzon Place.

♦ ♦ ♦

**Daniel W. Powell** teaches a variety of writing courses at Florida State College at Jacksonville. He is an avid outdoorsman and enjoys fishing the tidal creeks of Duval County from atop his kayak. His stories have appeared in *Redstone Science Fiction*, *Well Told Tales*, *Leading Edge Magazine*, *Brain Harvest*, *Something Wicked*, *Dead But Dreaming 2* and *Weber: The Contemporary West*.

Daniel shares a small house near the Intracoastal Waterway with his wife, Jeanne, and his daughter, Lyla. His journal on speculative storytelling can be found at www.danielwpowell.blogspot.com.

# "She's a Liquid"

by Ever Dundas
(for Cinnamon Curtis)

*Hurt*

He heard their voices first. They broke his reverie, and he sat up, looking at his watch. They emerged from the trees by the path. As he made to stand up, the first blow came.

These senseless seconds, unfolding in ease and simplicity.

The kick to the face sent him down, his blood spattering across the leaves of a tree.

They all laughed as he lay in the grass, spitting out teeth. They dragged him up, unsteady on his feet, hands raised in supplication.

*Dear Darkness*

The TV flickered. She began each morning with Nine Inch Nails live sets. The music and the lights helped her concentrate, to manage the pain. She could distinguish each pixel, each block of light. The pain would break up. It would become scattered, like the light, pulsing in and out. She thought she could control it.

She lost her focus, the light and pain merging. She was whole again, fixed, stable, made entirely from inflamed nerves. She let out a shocked breath, as if she had been punched in the chest.

She watched as the lead guitarist picked at the strings, as he slid his hand across the frets. She thought of how the strings must feel on his skin. She tried to imagine, closing her eyes, trying to feel a sensation she had never experienced. All she could think of was how her skin would have broken and blistered, how she would have drawn blood. She watched Reznor, staring at his skin as his muscles flexed. She felt the rhythm, she felt his smooth words. His voice was sex.

She was untouchable. Sometimes she ran her fused and scarred fingers over herself. Glimmers of pleasure in masochistic perversion.

She was to be good, she was to be pure. Sexless, but sexed.

Her skin precluded a daily beauty regime, but she still engaged in more than the routine of lancing blisters, antiseptic, and new bandages. She would style her hair, apply what make-up she could. She would float on a morphine haze, taking pride in the care it took to meet that daily performance, that presentation of self.

Sometimes she didn't feel anything at all.

She experienced different kinds of pain, on different days. Once, after refusing the morphine, she passed out. She woke up on the kitchen floor. The honey jar had fallen from the counter and smashed, honey and glass mingling with her blood. Her face was a raw mess from hitting the table as she fell. Her lip had split open.

She pushed herself up onto her elbows. She licked up the honey and the blood. She wanted to eat the glass. She wanted to eat the glass and drown in her own blood. She wanted to drown.

Liquid was her favourite thing. Liquid was her pleasure. Music was her liquid. It slithered over her, covering her like a second skin.

She felt her body was weighted down. It was her. She was it. She folded back into her body in an eternal torsion.

She had good days and bad days. Good hours and bad hours. Sometimes she lived by the second. Each second tick-tocked, good pain, bad pain, tolerable pain, pass-out pain.

Pain is pain is pain.

She was the hazy disappearance of time in a morphine cradle.

She wondered why the seconds didn't fold back in on themselves.

*We're in This Together*

She wanted to be alert today. She took the minimum amount of morphine needed to get through the hours it took to change her bandages. Dressed, she stood considering herself in the hallway mirror. Her blonde hair was styled, streaked through with blue. She had managed to draw in eyebrows without breaking the skin. She pretended the healing wounds on her face didn't matter. All that mattered was that they were healing, and she was coping. Her ears were filled with piercings, her nose, eyebrow, lips. She had suffered for it, but it was her choice.

She decided to walk to work, hoping the skin on her feet would survive the short distance. Rolling up her sleeve, she scrolled through the menu of the Endostream embedded in her wrist and selected Harvey's 'White Chalk'. Three small buttons lay smooth along the skin, glinting like tiny surface piercings. The rest of the Endo was positioned just below, the menu glowing a faint blue.

She had invented the Endostream. As a research fellow she had explored the relationship between the body, technology, and music. She won awards and was granted funding to advance music technology. From both her own experience and her research, she had a wealth of material on the healing properties of music. She transformed this into hard science, plugging it directly into the body, connecting it to the nerves.

When it hit the market, there was an explosion of media interest in her life. Articles, dripping in condescension, focused on her disability.

She was 'brave', 'courageous', an 'inspiration to us all.'

But she was also a freak, the embodiment of illness and broken down boundaries, a walking death.

Every journalist assumed she was single, and baulked when she told them she had a partner. They had been together since their teens, best friends, lovers, colleagues.

He became the poster boy. He was handsome, he had a winning smile. He wasn't covered in open sores.

They retreated, they continued as before.

They worked together on further music research, able to focus entirely on their work without worrying about money. The rest of her income was put straight into research on genetic skin disorders.

Then her priorities shifted.

Her whole life shifted.

Everything shifted, except time.

Time continued, inexorably linear.

She wondered why the seconds didn't fold back in on themselves.

*Closer*

She heard their voices first. They emerged from the trees by the path. He heard them too. They broke his reverie, and he sat up, looking at his watch. As he made to stand up, the first blow came.

These senseless seconds, unfolding in ease and simplicity.

The kick to the face sent him down, his blood spattering across her body.

As he lay in the grass, spitting out teeth, they all laughed.

She tried to reach him, her feet dragging through the grass as if she was weighted down. They began to flicker, as if she was watching them on a screen.

She could hear a low vibrating hum as they dragged him up. He was unsteady on his feet, hands raised in supplication.

*I Do Not Want This*

The morning research had gone badly. She thought a breakthrough had been reached, but it had come to nothing.

Her disappointment and anger exacerbated the pain.

Sitting in the canteen, she sipped at her liquidized lunch. She couldn't risk solid food, as her throat was still healing from the last attempt. Inside and outside. Always going through the process of healing and scarring and breaking apart again.

She overheard her name being mentioned at the table behind her.

"Luke says she's trying to make a time machine."

"You're kidding."

"No. She just holes herself up, doing 'research'. They only put up with her because of all the money she brings to the university, but she just lost it. There should be some sort of intervention, but no one cares as long as they get the money."

The gossip, the disappointment, and the pain all nagged at her. She put the music back on to drown them out, and to give her the hope that she would manage without more drugs.

But it didn't drown them out, it just enclosed their words in her head.

She still couldn't shake the anxiety, her mind going over and over what went wrong.

She felt her body scrunch up with rage, always folding in on herself. The music shifted to a low vibrating hum, and she slammed down her hand. Her skin shimmered, breaking apart, like liquid. It fell over the table in droplets, reformed and disappeared.

She stared at her hand, the anxiety increasing. Small scratches criss-crossed the surface of the table where the droplets had fallen. She wondered if she was going mad.

Looking across the cafeteria she saw a couple staring at her.

She was used to this. Her skin made her untouchable, but open to interrogation. People would ask 'what's wrong with you?' Some would laugh at her. Or feel sorry for her. Some would feel unease or repulsion.

The sick are sick. A perversion, a contagion. She wondered if she was a metaphor. She wondered if she was death.

She watched them as they peered at her, as they ate their lunch and strained their necks to see her. She watched them as they whispered.

She went over to the canteen counter, picking up crisps. Shoveling them in, she opened up the lining of her mouth, her throat. She tasted blood. Blood and salt.

She bared her teeth, sticking out her tongue. Blood-crisps dripped to the floor.

She watched the reaction of the couple who were staring.

Some people would feel unease and repulsion.

*Before Departure*

Swallowing blood, she slumped into her office chair. She contemplated morphine, contemplated A&E.

Instead she put the neural helmet on, resuming work.

She was exhausted. She counted the years since his death. She had worked on this obsessively. Every time it failed, she reminded herself that his life depended on it. Her life depended on it. But this obsession was only delaying the inevitable. She couldn't live without him, and time travel was a dream.

Forever delayed, she wondered why the seconds didn't fold.

She turned up the music, listening to the song they had listened to all those years ago. Her blood fell, an incessant beat. The music responded, notes dripping in perfect time. The rhythm was hypnotic, a metallic clink as the blood hit her hands.

The computer responded as the neural helmet picked up her brain's electromagnetic fields. Adjusting the settings of her experiment, she set the programme running and waited.

The rhythm shifted, broken up by syncopation, a doubling of speed. The notes fell with her blood in a disjointed collage. Time contracted.

*Beside You in Time*

She awoke. A slow waking, limbs stretching lazily, eyelids opening and closing. She felt the warmth of the sun on her skin. And there was no pain.

Her eyes opened.

Her body unfurled, her skin shimmering. She unfurled, and there was no pain. As she moved, the music responded, shifting between chords. It faded in and out, following the rhythm of her body.

It soothed her. Liquid exoskeleton elixir.

She stood, contemplating her new skin. Running her fingers across her arm, the music pulsated. Her skin danced over her fingers, cold and soothing. Droplets fell on to the pavement, rolling and merging, snaking their way back to her and crawling up her leg until they disappeared into the flow.

She wondered if this was a morphine dream.

She wondered if she was in heaven.

Someone approached her, brushing past, knocking her skin and setting off the music in an arrhythmic jangle. Her skin burst open and fell in a shower, before collecting on the pavement and joining her again as the music evened out.

She was near the riverbank. She hadn't been here since his death. Everything looked the same.

And then she saw herself.

Down by the river. She sat with him, just as they had been all those years ago.

She crept down to the river. They didn't acknowledge her as she approached. She sat next to them, but they didn't see her.

They were listening to the song she had become, the piano notes flowing, soothing. They held hands, and he leaned his head on her shoulder.

She longed to touch him. She wondered if he would feel it, if he would feel her new skin, if she could touch him and no longer feel pain. But when she approached him, her skin just fell apart, tumbling to the grass and snaking its way back to her.

And then she watched herself kiss him goodbye and leave.

She remembered this. This was seared into her. This moment had haunted her for years. This moment, these seconds.

She fell to her knees. She told him to leave, but he heard nothing. He leaned back, resting on the palms of his hands, turning his face to the fading sun.

She watched herself walk away, and she thought of all the years it had taken her to come back here. All these years, and all it was to her was spectacle. She thought how perverse it was that she had worked so hard only to witness his death.

She wondered if she was in hell.

She tried over and over to touch him, to move him. She shouted at him, her yell disappearing into the music, her impotence echoed by the silent beat that broke the rhythm.

She sat with him as he lay back on the grass, dreaming, floating. She sat with him, listening to her music-skin.

She heard their voices first. The music shifted to a heavy arpeggio as they emerged from the trees by the path. He heard them too. They broke his reverie, and he sat up, looking at his watch. As he made to stand up, the first blow came.

These senseless seconds, unfolding in ease and simplicity.

The kick to the face sent him down, his blood spattering across her body, exploding the music in a fury.

They all laughed, and the music became a low vibrating hum as the droplets returned to her.

He lay in the grass, spitting out teeth. They dragged him up, unsteady on his feet, hands raised in supplication. They punched him, and he was down again.

She watched them as they took pleasure in those seconds before they moved in on him. She felt the spark of expectation. She remembered the report. She remembered what they had done to him.

As they circled him, her music-skin churned in rage. She collided with them, her skin fragmenting.

Small slivers of music-skin sliced into them. The music retained a steady rhythm, a gentle soprano drifting over the piano. With precision, skin was flayed. The fine blades of music-skin hit one of the assailants with such force that veins were torn from his arm.

Now she was Hades. A liquid mellifluous death.

They lay at her feet, stripped of their skin.

Kneeling down, she enveloped him. The droplets of music-skin returned to her and flowed over him.

She was poison-cure. The great destroyer, the great healer.

In this twilight, the music hummed.

*She's a Liquid*

Her favourite food is honey. It slithers down her throat. When they kiss, they pass it back and forth.

Pressing the button in her wrist, she becomes music. She folds in on herself in an eternal torsion, her skin flowing in rivulets.

Music is her liquid exoskeleton elixir.

They kiss, and there is no pain.

**Ever Dundas** is a writer and artist living in Edinburgh. She recently graduated with a Creative Writing Masters with Distinction from Edinburgh Napier University. Her interests include Queer Theory, and the relationship between humans, animals, and technology.

She keeps a blog at:
bloodonforgottenwalls.wordpress.com/

# "Aftershocks"

by Craig D.B. Patton

He checks his watch. 05-23-10 4:15 A.M. He shows his wife. She nods and tightens her grip on his hand to stop the trembling. Their son will be home again very soon.

It has been four years since their son vanished in a massive truck bomb explosion in Baghdad. Witnesses said he was standing right next to it when it went off.

There was an empty, flag-draped casket at the funeral. Framed photos everywhere, overcompensating for the lack of a body. A field's worth of flowers. Well wishes and military salutes. Then tail lights receding down the long dirt road from their home and a settling, spreading emptiness.

For weeks, they remained deep in shock. Sometimes they even believed their son still lived. The casket flag and the condolence letter from the President in the family room reminded them otherwise.

The swelling boil of their grief ruptured on their son's birthday in July. They wailed. They smashed dishes. They screamed at God. How could He take their son? They had prayed every day for his safety. He had been a pious man, respectful and humble, eager to do good in this troubled world.

God did not answer.

On the first anniversary of their son's death, they were not at home. They had gone to her sister's home in Minneapolis, seeking comfort from family.

When they returned, they opened the front door and stared. The living room was trashed. Paintings hung askew or lay on the floor. The mirror and lamp were shattered. Plants were toppled, spilling dirt onto the floor.

They called the police.

Nothing was stolen. But that was only the beginning of the mystery. There was no sign of forced entry. There were no fingerprints. No evidence of an intruder at all except in the living room.

They felt worse when the police left. But, as the passing days turned into weeks and months, they forgot about the incident.

A tremendous concussion awoke them in the predawn of the following May 23$^{rd}$. They thought the furnace had exploded. They hurried downstairs, certain that their house was on fire.

It was not. But the living room had been wrecked again and, again, the door was intact and locked.

Unsure what else to do, the wife picked up their new clock from where it lay on the floor. It was broken, the hands stopped at 4:17 A.M. Her breath hissed out. She knew that time well. She showed her husband. His eyes widened. He knew it just as well.

It was the second anniversary of their son's death. He had died at 11:17 A.M. in Baghdad. 4:17 A.M. where they lived.

They did not call the police. Instead, together, they turned on all of the lights in the house. Then they brewed coffee and sat at the kitchen table, where they had all of their serious conversations.

They were frightened. What was happening was not easily explained. And the idea that it was connected to their son disturbed them. But that very connection made it irresistible. They wanted, *needed* to understand it.

Their son's tour would have ended in three days. They had spoken to him the night before he died. Wasn't it possible, they asked each other, that he was thinking about home, about them, when the bomb took him wherever he went? And might that be the source of this annual event? Didn't it make some sense, given what stood in for logic when contemplating the incomprehensible?

They waited a very long year to find out.

Their alarm woke them at 4:00 A.M. the following May 23rd. They put on their robes, went downstairs, and sat on the couch in the living room, facing the door. They waited, feeling a bit frightened, a bit foolish. But they were also a bit hopeful. They might, they had told each other, finally have a chance to see their son again.

At 4:17 A.M., the husband's watch beeped. Seconds later, a figure appeared just inside the door. It was their son, from shaved head to combat boots, but it was like looking at a worn out film projection of him. Parts of his uniform and face were blurred. There were scratches and tears. They could see the door through them.

The wife started to call out to her son, but there was no time.

They saw his head twitch, as if he had just started to turn it. Then the figure that was all that was left of their son vanished in the opposite direction, as though a great wind had gusted him away.

There was an overwhelming noise. Like a single clap of thunder right in the room. Like God smashing a mountain. Everything went black.

When they woke, they were both bleeding from the ears and nose. One of the windows was broken. A crack ran half way up a wall.

The bleeding stopped. They could hear. They didn't want to go to the hospital. Didn't want to answer unanswerable questions. Instead, they sat there amid the damage. They held each other and cried.

Eventually, they cleaned up and, when May came again, they were ready.

The windows are boarded up. The clock and paintings and plants have been removed. They are wearing ear plugs and ear muffs and nose clips.

And now the father's watch beeps. It is 4:17 A.M.

Time to welcome their son home again.

**Craig D.B. Patton**'s stories and poems have appeared in *Wily Writers, Shroud Magazine*, *A Sea of Alone: Poems for Alfred Hitchcock* (Dark Scribe Press), and other markets. He's a member of the New England Horror Writers Association, and you'll find that he blogs at flawedcreations.wordpress.com, where he hopes to hear from you.

# "Outsourced"

## by Shelly Li

The sign in the window says: "Offering Jobs to Non-Humans Only."

Oh my God, I think as I trudge along the street, walking and walking to find an employer that will hire a human. It's been three months since the big outsourcing plan was put into place at Microsoft, three months since I'd even seen the inside of a corporate building.

I let out a deep breath, watch the cold smoke seep from my lips and spread out into the Chicago air. What if I never find a job again?

"Hey, watch it!" a voice bleeds into my ear.

I blink to clear the haze out of my eyes and notice that I've run into someone. "Sorry," I say to the alien — I'm not sure what planet he's from — and move back from the inside of his coat, taking my hands off his blue-colored chest. "I didn't…"

I stop all of a sudden and look down at the tips of my fingers. "Paint…?"

It takes a few seconds for the meaning of this to sink in for me, but when it finally does, I feel the tightening pain in my chest disappear. "Oh my God," I say, looking up at Mr. Blue Paint. "You're …you're a human …aren't you?"

A terrified scowl drops over his face like a curtain, and he pushes past me and hurries away.

I turn around and watch as he moves through the people around him, amazed. How can this be? I wonder. Has no one caught him yet?

I don't know the answers to these questions, but what I do know is that if I don't give this man's idea a try, I will not be able to feed my family for much longer.

♦

The interviewer is half-human, half-alien, but with a black overcoat covering her body, the only thing that differentiates her from a full human are the golden spots cast across her forehead.

"So," she says, smiling at me with a row of perfect teeth. "Tell me, Mr. Alimano, what is your family history?"

"Well, I was born here in Chicago. My mother emigrated to Earth from Sennia when she was just a few centuries old. When my father came to Earth on business from Polum a couple millennia later, he and my mother were wed. They gave birth to me a few years later."

The interviewer nodded and pointed to my orange-red hands. "I can see that your mother has given you flexible Sennian fingers," she says. "Those will be perfect for typing. What's your speed?"

My heart freezes then, for I do not know the normal typing speed of an alien. "Nine hundred words a minute," I decide to say after a little pause.

"Hmm. That sounds a little low for a Sennian, but…" She shrugs and writes "900" down on the notepad in front of her. "You are only 50% of your mother. It's probably reasonable."

She looks up at me, her black eyes piercing into mine, drowning me in a dark abyss. "Mr. Alimano," she says. "You're hired. Can you start tomorrow?"

♦

The job is not as hard as I thought it would be. As long as I keep under the radar, socialize at a minimum with my co-workers, and work hard, I am sure that I will stay employed.

Slowly, winter turns to spring, then fades into summer. Summer rolls into autumn, and before I know it, winter is here again. But now my family is living with a roof over their heads and food in their stomachs — perhaps I will even buy Christmas gifts for Nicky and Joel this year, or maybe take a little vacation.

"Hey," my boss walks up and says to me. He once told me that he was from Lotruus, the desert planet, which is why his skin is so green and tough. "Have you typed up the shipment schedule for Sector Seven yet?"

"Yes." I reach over and grab the schedule from the printer, but my arm does not extend far enough. My boss chuckles. "Don't worry," he says, and reaches over me. "I'll grab it." But his elbow rubs up against my face as he pulls back, and the tingly texture of his skin is too much for me to handle. I sneeze.

For a moment, my boss says nothing, merely stares at me with those piercing eyes of his. Then he glances down at his arm.

I don't understand why he is acting this way until I look down and see the blood mixed in with the snot on his arm. "This is the blood of a human," my boss says to me. "Isn't it?" I keep quiet, and we lapse into silence yet again. Shivers are rolling through my body, but I can do nothing to stop them.

I can hear my heart pounding, louder and louder, almost threatening to burst out of my chest when finally, my boss leans in and whispers to me: "You fix this...ailment of yours, okay? This encounter of ours did not happen."

I nod, not even daring to breathe.

"Merry Christmas," he says, and walks away.

**Shelly Li** is a freshman at Duke. Beginning in 2009, she has published over 20 short stories in places such as *Nature*, *Cosmos*, and *Daily Science Fiction*. Her most well-known work, "The Parachute," won the national gold medal in Scholastic's Art & Writing Awards. Shelly's first novel of YA Fantasy, *The Royal Hunter*, will be out from Philomel Books (Penguin Group). For more information, please visit: www.shelly-li.com.

# "Absolution"

by Matt Adams

Absolution believed in angels and the power of the divine.

They had shaped him.

A lifetime ago, he had been Connor O'Riley, a bartender at an Irish establishment of good standing within his community. Like the other men and women in his family, he enjoyed the company of a stiff drink and the driving music of the Dropkick Murphys.

Saturdays were for the Fighting Irish.

Sundays were for mass.

In his mid-twenties, Connor O'Riley became no more.

It began in a dark alley behind the bar where he and his family celebrated the ups and downs of life; the victories and disappointments of the Irish football team, the confirmations and weddings, the wakes with smoke-filled rooms packed with mourners.

He'd witnessed two men drag a woman out into the street. They beat her, their words carrying the foreboding nature of what would happen next. Connor wouldn't allow it. And, either kissed by the effects of too many shots or carried on the wings of angels, he set upon the men.

He wasn't much of a fighter back then; wasn't much of anything, really.

And the men laughed and cavorted and stabbed him more times than Connor's mind was capable of counting.

*Cold.*

His teeth chattered and his body shook, the cobblestone around him washed in his own blood. He remembered the woman's scream for help, recalled the piercing sound of police cars and the ambulance.

*Bright.*

He awoke covered in tubes and bandages.

He felt nothing.

The doctors and nurses said they admired his strength and his fortitude. They commented on his remarkable recovery, adding that Connor must've been blessed by a higher power.

Unable to move his arms and legs, Connor wondered how anyone could consider him blessed.

*Dark.*

His mother and father stood at his bedside. The tubes and bandages became fewer and fewer, and Connor's breath came with comforting ease.

His mother placed a hand upon his shoulder and Connor felt it.

He wiggled his fingers and tried to flex his toes.

Nothing.

His parents told him they loved him.

*Overcast.*

They wheeled him up to the front with the rest of the O'Riley family.

All dressed in black, except for his father. He'd requested burial with his Notre Dame Monogram Club jacket.

Lightning pulsed through the sky, punctuated with authoritative cracks of thunder. Cold needles splashed across Connor's shoulders.

Warm tears streaked down his cheeks.

*Golden.*

He rose on steady feet for the first time in ages, unencumbered by the wheeled monstrosity that bound him to earth.

A dream.

A fantasy.

A revelation.

"*Child of God, ye be wronged,*" a thousand harmonious voices soothed.

Connor couldn't blink, couldn't speak.

He observed.

Golden light.

The outline of billowing wings belonging to a pure, beautiful face in front of him.

Neither man nor woman.

Celestial.

"*A world rife with pain and suffering. It displeases the Father.*"

Connor felt a tickle in the back of his throat and tried to speak.

He felt the energy of celestial hands upon his face.

"What would you have me do?" he asked.

"*Not us. He,*" the voices responded. "*The Sword. Thou art the Sword.*"

Connor didn't understand.

"I'm not trained…"

A thousand pure laughs reverberated.

"*Not a literal sword, child. The Sword.*"

Connor held out his hands, "I do not understand."

The wings quickened their smooth rippling.

*"Perhaps He was mistaken."*

The voices seemed conciliatory.

Connor dropped to his knees, "I will do that which is required."

*"Not revenge, child. Justice. Protect those in need. Silence the corrupt. Thou shalt see their wickedness in their fear. Provide them with Absolution, for that is thy name."*

*Emptiness.*

The angelic figure was no more.

Connor sat inside the building that once housed a loving family. Memories lined the walls. A once-vibrant championship banner hung, its glory faded through the years.

Connor strangled the arms of his wheelchair.

*Gone.*

*All of them.*

Only he remained.

*Powerless.*

*Frail.*

His nerve endings exploded with an energy he hadn't felt in months. Hands trembling, he pushed himself up, his jelly legs bowing from inutility and fatigue.

*Feeling.*

He dropped to his knees and prayed.

His Creator had provided him with a second chance.

He would provide the wicked with Absolution.

◆

He required no rehabilitation following his revelation, but Absolution needed training. Firearms, explosives, and knives were the tools of his second chance. And so he fashioned two firearms—one black and one white—that saw the world as their creator did.

Research dominated his training regimen and Absolution had learned much. Of all the dregs within his crumbling city, the Callahan crime family loomed largest. That they fenced stolen merchandise did not bother him; that they laundered money and dabbled in black-market electronics was unimportant. Their larger transgressions could not be ignored. They trafficked in prostitution and drugs, pleasured in killing, and corrupted the police with their tainted ideals.

The Callahan's current operation involved the importation of black-market merchandise at the docks. The manifest claimed electronics; Absolution guessed drugs.

White foam splashed across the pier and a distant, burly figure pulled its coat tighter.

*Kevin "Big Irish" Callahan.*

*Oldest of the brothers.*

*Not the brightest.*

Absolution recognized others in the dim light; the two other Callahan brothers—Tommy and Jimmy—and one of their many cousins.

*Patrick O'Toole.*

*Violent.*

*Uncontrollable.*

The four figures gathered around a rusted shipping container. "Big Irish" Callahan tore the door open.

*Not the brightest.*

The explosion shook the pier, and Absolution steadied himself.

Four members of the Callahan crime family lay motionless as smoke curled into the air.

He would provide Absolution.

♦

"We have only a few minutes before the police arrive," Absolution said softly.

Jimmy Callahan's lips quivered.

*Fear.*

*Boozing with his brothers at the age of 16.*

*Sleeping with his sweetheart in their mid-teens.*

*Feeling the cool steel of a new gun.*

Absolution collapsed as the images flashed through his mind.

♦

A soothing voice filled his memory, *"Silence the corrupt. Thou shalt see their wickedness in their fear."*

Absolution understood.

He rose.

♦

For a youngster, Jimmy Callahan's sins were great. The capacity for wickedness and corruptness existed within the youngest brother. Absolution thought his transgressions unworthy of his time.

He turned toward "Big Irish" Callahan.

Larger than his brother Jimmy, Kevin Callahan's imposing frame posed a much different threat. Absolution leapt atop him.

The young man's half-burned face held the fetid stench of rotten, overcooked steak.

Absolution shook the oldest brother, "Where is it coming from?"

Big Irish grimaced; Absolution guessed it was a smile.

"Isn't talkin' to no one," Big Irish said, steel behind his words.

Absolution bounced Big Irish's head hard enough to splinter the creaking wooden pier. He drew out one of his pistols and Big Irish's eyes widened.

*Thou shalt see their wickedness in their fear.*

Images assaulted him…

*Hanging a butcher inside his own refrigerator.*

*Giving his underage brothers a case of beer.*

*Forcing Vito Gambino's head into the water at the docks, letting go only after the man stopped waving his arms.*

*Invading a home with his brother Tommy and cousin Patrick.*

Absolution steadied himself on a nearby pillar.

The final image seemed familiar. He pointed the gun at Big Irish again, but fire flashed in the man's eyes. His fear had subsided.

Absolution turned toward Patrick O'Toole. The cousin was relatively unscathed, with only a few burn marks singeing his leather coat.

"You're a holy man," Patrick said as he sat up on his elbows. "What with the big red cross there and all. Mark of the Templars, right? I thought the pope burned those heretics a few hundred years ago."

Absolution regarded the crimson cross that adorned his dark body armor. He'd chosen it for its symmetry. That it also represented the Templars did not occur to him.

Patrick laughed, "Don't even know what you're doing, do ya? Messing with the Callahans? My uncle don't take kindly to anyone messing with his boys. Or his nephew."

The young man smiled, a crazed look overtaking his face, "The city couldn't survive without the Callahans and the O'Tooles. Think about that."

The young man was not afraid.

Absolution grabbed the cousin by his leather coat and thrust him into the water.

Gurgled protests followed.

Absolution smiled.

*Playing Russian roulette with a family rival and taking the empty gun for his own.*

*Delivering Cuban cigars and cash to the police department.*

*Invading a home where a faded championship banner hung.*

Absolution pulled Patrick from the water and tossed him next to Big Irish. He leveled both pistols at the men.

"Tell me about the deaths of the O'Riley family," Absolution rasped.

A sloppy, hearty laugh escaped Big Irish's mouth.

Patrick followed suit.

The other brothers continued lying down.

"The O'Rileys? Those deadbeats?" Patrick asked.

Absolution delivered a sharp blow with his black pistol.

He was about to strike again when the clouds parted to reveal overwhelming, golden light.

"What are you staring at?" Big Irish grumbled.

"He's gone batty, cousin," Patrick said.

Absolution did not hear them.

♦

The face. Beautiful. Celestial.

"Why have you returned? I am providing absolution," he said.

Tears streamed down the cherubic face.

*"Not revenge, child. Justice."*

"These men killed my family…"

The angelic form's wings billowed gracefully, obscuring the golden light from above. It tilted its head and gazed with understanding eyes.

*"Tools of your family's demise. They have done great evil. Thou art the Sword. Strike them down with only the purest of intentions. Not revenge. Never revenge. Justice for what they have done to prevent that which they could do. Reveal to them the Glory. Provide them with Absolution."*

The figure narrowed its compassionate eyes, *"Their transgressions are supreme. Remember they are but tools of thy family's demise. Tools, not those who wielded them."*

The clouds swallowed the radiant light, leaving behind only the faint onrushing of the choppy waters.

♦

An uneasy tingle ran down Absolution's spine.

"You killed them. I know this," he said, moving his guns among all four members of the Callahan family. "You must confess your sins."

"I don't see a holy book or a rosary or a confessional booth. To hell with you."

The voice came from Tommy.

Absolution turned, "Tommy Callahan. You have thrown your lot in with your older brother and detestable cousin. You do not seem afraid."

"If my family weren't lying in heaps of pain right now, you would be," Tommy retorted.

Absolution ran a gloved hand over a small scar on Tommy's right cheek.

"What would your father think of you?" he asked. "Following your stupid older brother? Botching a family operation?"

Absolution turned his eyes upward, concentrating on a distant sound: the din of approaching sirens.

"The police will arrive soon," he said, leaning closer to Tommy. "But they won't find much."

Tommy swallowed, and Absolution closed his eyes.

*Forcing his girlfriend to do unimaginable things to him at the barrel of a gun.*

*Cutting a bartender with a broken bottle after refusing to pay for his drink.*

*Setting fire to Mr. Smith's home after the principal suspended him from the basketball team.*

*Drawing up plans for an assault on the O'Riley house.*

Absolution stumbled away from Tommy and regained his bearings.

*Not revenge. Justice.*

Familiar words passed across his lips; he could not recall where they came from.

"I love my neighbor as myself for the love of Thee. I forgive all who have injured me."

Three of the men shouted apologies for their various transgressions.

The youngest, Jimmy, remained silent.

He clicked back the hammer, "And ask pardon of all whom I have injured."

Three shots echoed through the pier.

"Go and tell them," he said, holstering his pistols as Jimmy trembled. "They will not find absolution. Absolution will find them."

♦

He dug for months, maybe a year, tracking down the lower associates of the Callahan crime family and preying on their fears to silence the corrupt.

They led him straight to Jimmy Callahan, Senior.

He approached the ancient, crumbling cathedral where the man conjured his criminal plans. Saint Mark's Catholic Church had been supplanted by a larger, more ornate building a few blocks away. The original Saint Mark's remained, protected by the "historical landmark" designation and the patronage of Jimmy Senior.

Absolution crouched and admired the dark asymmetry of the church's double steeples. The stone exterior gave off a dull shine in the moonlight, and the building remained dark save for a single light.

He entered.

♦

"Not taking on boys this time," Jimmy Senior said, slapping Absolution across the face.

Two sets of well-muscled arms held him in place.

Jimmy Senior ran a hand through his unkempt hair, so fiery red it may as well have been orange.

"I heard about you," the man said, the faint tinge of an Irish accent in his voice. He'd passed down the vocal legacy to his sons. "Jimmy told me about you. Coming to the docks to disrupt a Callahan family operation. We're just simple merchants, my boy."

Jimmy Senior kneed Absolution in the stomach.

"That's the strangest cross I ever saw," he said with a laugh that shook his ragged cheeks.

The old man paced across the small, carpeted office floor. "Now why are you here? I've seen your face before. Connor isn't it? Been a while. Funeral on wheels?"

Absolution stayed still.

"Your family ran into some bad luck, I suppose," Jimmy Senior said, showing Absolution his back. "You being all heroic and getting maimed by those kids. I ran them out of town. No place for animals like that in our city."

The old man picked up a silver offering plate and spun it in his hands, "It wasn't supposed to be a massacre, lad. It really wasn't. But people like your folks pay for protection. And when they're late with their payments, it makes it easy for others to do the same."

Jimmy Senior sat the plate aside and turned on his heels, "My boys were sent to give them a scare. It was a rite of passage for Tommy. Little Jimmy wasn't old enough for that kind of work. Those hospital bills of yours were piling up. They weren't paying. We had to do something."

Absolution shook his shoulders in a vain effort to escape the iron grips that held him in place.

Jimmy Senior placed a hand on Absolution's shoulder, "It wasn't supposed to end like that. But I understand. I take your family, you take mine. But not all blood weighs the same, lad. You must be punished."

"Not revenge. Justice," Absolution said.

"So he speaks," Jimmy Senior mocked.

A slender figure entered the small office.

"Jimmy, what are you doing here?" the old man said, tugging on his hooded sweatshirt.

The young man sulked into the room with his hands in his pockets. Red-rimmed eyes and poorly-concealed sniffles gave him away.

"He took them, Dad," the boy said.

*Steel behind his words. Like Big Irish.*

The boy took his hands out of his pockets and stiffened, "Let me kill him."

Jimmy Senior put a hand on his son's shoulders, his eyes threatening to burst.

"No, son."

The younger Jimmy drew in a deep breath. The boy stood a good four inches taller than his father.

Jimmy Junior swallowed, "My brothers are dead because of him. My cousin…"

Jimmy Senior placed his hands on the side of his son's face, "You weren't responsible…"

"Dad, I just sat there," the boy said, his voice cracking. "I should be with them."

Absolution felt for the boy.

He could yet be redeemed.

The hired muscle loosened their grip enough for Absolution to slip one arm out. A sharp elbow and a kick later, both were down, and Absolution grabbed one of their guns. Two loud bursts filled the small office, followed by two identical moans of pain.

"Your sins are great, Jimmy Callahan," Absolution said, pointing the revolver at the old man. "Your progeny are infected with your lust for power and money. God does not approve."

"I'm not afraid of you," Jimmy Senior said.

Even with the gun trained on him, the old man remained strong.

Absolution's eyes shifted toward Jimmy Junior, as did his weapon.

Jimmy Senior thrust himself in front of his son.

Absolution felt it.

*Fear.*

*Shaking down local merchants for protection money and using it to buy off local authorities.*

*Removing the blade from a traitorous associate and dumping the body by the docks.*

*Bringing Father Joseph a young woman from the congregation.*

*Receiving orders directly from the priest.*

The last image nearly brought Absolution to his knees.

"Go," Absolution said, pointing with his gun for the boy to leave.

The boy stood in place.

"GO!" Absolution yelled.

Jimmy Senior gently pushed his son toward the back door.

"Go," he whispered. "My sins have caught up with me. Don't let yours do the same."

He stood on his tiptoes to leave a wet kiss on the boy's cheek and closed the door.

"I have seen your great evils, Jimmy Callahan. Yet, I sense you are nothing more than a tool."

Brightness poured into the room.

♦

Serene.

Sad.

Celestial.

*"Child, bring justice."*

The winged form paused for an instant, its feathered wings coming to a stop.

When the heavenly host said no more, Absolution spoke, "This man has done terrible things. But he is a tool of a greater evil. An evil closer to our Lord."

*"This man is wicked. Thou art the Sword. Silence the corrupt."*

"The corrupt are of God. I have seen it."

A hand on his face.

Warmth.

Empowerment.

*"The soul you speak of cannot be touched. He is protected."*

'Protected? By whom?"

*"By us. By Him. He swore an oath."*

Absolution knelt, "He broke his oath. He is corrupt. He must be punished. I am the Sword."

Streams of golden tears.

A look of concern.

Pity.

*"To provide Absolution would rob thy Creator of his Final Justice. Dost thou wish so?"*

The angelic form now dwarfed Absolution, who continued kneeling.

"I do not wish to anger the Father," he said, his eyes downcast. He looked up, "But I do not agree on this matter. The world is a better place without such men, more so if they pretend to serve the Father."

A ripple of even brighter light.

Strains of distant music.

A thunderclap.

*"Thou art the Sword. Silence the corrupt. Beware of hidden demons."*

♦

"You gone mental, kid?" Jimmy Senior said in his Irish twinge, bringing Absolution back to earth.

The old man stood closer, but Absolution kept the gun trained on him.

He began reciting his prayer and gestured for Jimmy Senior to fall to his knees. The old man complied, and Absolution could see the top of his red head, so bright it flared like fire.

Two shots later, Jimmy Callahan, Senior, lay dead on the floor's faded carpet.

Absolution retrieved the firearms that had been clumsily thrown on the office desk and headed for the new St. Mark's Catholic Church.

◆

"I am not afraid of you," Father Joseph said. "I am a man of God. You are a murderer. Thou shalt not kill."

"I am the Sword, father. I answer to a higher power," Absolution responded.

"As do I," Father Joseph said, holding a ragged Bible to his chest.

"This church is built upon the blood of innocents. Tainted money from the Callahan family. You let them become monsters."

Father Joseph licked his lips, "Clearly, you are confused, my child. Perhaps we should pray…"

Absolution pointed his black-and-white pistols at the holy man, "I am commanded by angels. I will provide absolution."

Father Joseph laughed, "Absolution! Do you even know what that means? To forgive a man of the evils he has done. To take his soul from this wicked world and set him free! You're not punishing the wicked! You're saving them!"

Absolution's outstretched arms suddenly felt frail, shaky.

"Impossible," Absolution said. "I am the Sword."

The priest placed his Bible upon a lectern and stepped forward, tugging at his collar and smoothing out his wispy gray hair. The cathedral's interior seemed massive, its marble floor shining from dim overhead lighting.

"The newspapers tell of some phantom that haunts the Callahan family. They say this abomination has cleansed the streets of muck and filth. The people say, 'go forward!' It pleases the people."

"It pleases the Lord!" Absolution said, ignoring his quaking knees.

"You are in a House of God," the priest said, "brandishing tools of violence."

Absolution's eyes met the priest's.

He saw no fear.

Perhaps this was a man of God.

He laid his guns in front of himself and knelt.

♦

Heavy footsteps and the scraping of metal against the marble floor cut through the reverent silence.

The barrels of twin pistols—one white, one black—stared back at him.

*Beware of hidden demons.*

"How does it feel on the other end?" Father Joseph asked, holding the weapons with steady hands.

"I bless you for judging me worthy of this day, this hour, so that in the company of the martyrs I may share the cup of Christ," Absolution said, looking up to regard his captor.

Absolution tilted his head.

The indication was slight, nearly imperceptible.

But the steady hands that held his pistols began shaking.

*Fear.*

Absolution prepared himself for the onrush of sensations.

*A confession taken and then spread to other fathers during a night at the pub…*

*A priest who looked over his congregation with too much interest in one particular girl...*

*A Man of God complicit in murder.*

The priest held his hands steadier.

"Even the purest heart is not chaste, father," Absolution said, his tone gentle.

Father Joseph extended his arms and they began trembling more noticeably.

The older man swallowed, "An abomination. A heretic. You have no place at this altar."

Absolution rose, "I must continue. God wills it."

The priest's hands shook furiously and a thunderclap echoed throughout the church.

Absolution felt the warm, sticky moisture seep from his arm.

The priest collapsed to his knees and the firearms fell from his hands.

Absolution cradled them before they hit the floor.

He stepped forward, "I love my neighbor as myself for the love of Thee. I forgive all who have injured me."

He clicked back the hammer, "And ask pardon of all whom I have injured."

The cathedral shook again.

Absolution dropped a token in the donation box before leaving.

He would pray for Father Joseph.

♦

He emerged from the cathedral holding his arm. Uneven cobblestones made walking a chore, but Absolution endured.

He carefully removed his armored shell.

*My cross to bear.*

Absolution turned in an alley and footsteps echoed behind him.

A tall, wiry frame silhouetted in moonlight approached.

One shot ripped through his right arm.

Another through his shoulder.

His thigh.

And so on.

Absolution held his stomach with both hands.

A youthful face revealed itself.

*Beware of hidden demons.*

"You may have cleaned up the Callahans. But not all of them."

A flash-bang.

Then, nothing.

Now, Everything.

Soft, inviting wings flowed gracefully.

The face.

Beautiful.

Celestial.

*"We warned of hidden demons. Yet thou art here."*

"I am the Sword," Absolution said.

The form shook its head in an ethereal, wavy motion.

*"Thou were the Sword. There is another."*

"I am Absolution!" he said.

*"Thou art Connor."*

Warmth wrapped around Connor's body, and bright, golden rays cascaded from his eyes, arms, and legs.

He was one of them.

They were him.

A brighter flash of light.

He saw *as* the face.

A young, lanky figure stood before them.

Confused.

Isolated.

He spoke of revenge.

*"Not revenge, child,"* Connor and the infinite choir reminded, *"Justice."*

The boy rubbed his chin, "Who am I?"

Connor and the others smiled, *"Thou art no longer Jimmy Callahan. Thou art the Sword. Thou shalt provide Absolution."*

The boy seemed perplexed, and Connor offered a final piece of wisdom.

*"Beware of hidden demons."*

**Matt Adams** is a former TV news producer whose short stories have appeared in *Wily Writers for Speculative Fiction* and anthologies from Library of the Living Dead Press. His first novel, *I, Crimsonstreak*, is due out in May 2012 from Candlemark & Gleam. Matt lives and works in Indianapolis, Indiana, with his wife and (possibly) man-eating frog. You can find out more about his writing at mattadamsauthor.blogspot.com.

# "Grandmonster"

by Sasha Janel McBrayer

Gram kept her teeth in a glass at the sink. The water inside the glass distorted them. I never could look at them directly. When I had to pee, I'd pass them on tiptoes. Gram's mouth without her teeth inside frightened me, too. She wasn't Gram without her teeth inside her head. She was someone small, white, lined.

Gram would put her teeth back in her mouth on Thursday nights even though it was close to bedtime. She put loud yellow heels on for playing shuffleboard with her friends. Those high heels were loud on the eyes and loud on the old wood floor. She'd leave me home with the TV and with homework. She'd tell me "behave" but I'd steal from her secret hoard of baking chocolate the moment I heard her tires finish crunching the gravel outside.

Gram told me I mustn't steal. She told me to sit still at school and not to bring no attention to myself.

"You don't want to be no criminal," she used to say. "You don't want to wind up in jail like your father."

Gram's oldest son—my dad, he didn't steal nothing. He killed my mom.

One Thursday night I lost track of time. I was still watching the TV when Gram came home. I heard the door and those loud heels and then her shape was standing in the entrance way. In the dark, the glow from the set made everything yellow. She stood there, rigid, and I stopped breathing. I had stayed up too late. Gram had never punished me before. I behaved. I behaved because Gram's teeth in that glass frightened me. Gram shifted and I heard a single pop of one of those high heels on the floor.

"You get to bed now," she said. She was using her Saturday morning, "How you?" voice. The one she used to greet the other grand kids and kiss them on their rosy cheeks when they visited. It was mismatched in the dark. It was too sweet. As I sprinted past her to my bedroom, relieved, I saw something wet on Gram that wasn't there before. Even in the hazy, sour, yellow glow I knew it was blood. How could I sleep when I knew Gram was next door, wet with blood?

The next Thursday Gram didn't go to play shuffleboard. We went to the Bob Dryer funeral together instead. Bob used to play shuffleboard, too. The black dress I had to wear itched me.

The mailman went missing. Fritz had been Gram's mailman fifteen years. They stapled a flyer with his face on it to the power pole in front of the house. It asked, "Have you seen this man?"

When my stomach got upset Gram came into my room with a big ol' jar of dirt.

"Good ol' Kentucky clay from the back yard. It'll cure anythin'. Just you watch."

Gram rubbed it on my tummy and in a half an hour I was fine.

At dinner that night Gram's hand wavered. She dropped her fork. When I looked at her, she was frozen a long time, then said, "Daylight ain't f'r us t'fear. It's not just blood we drink. Hopes n' dreams n' intentions. Understand?"

I just stared at my grand-mother.

"It's why your dad couldn't resist your mom," she continued. "She was full of those. Lot's t' feed off of."

"Dirt from this land will cure anythin' that ails ya," she added with a sigh. "But we don't live forever. That's just part o' the myth. *I* won't live forever. You'll learn, though. Even half-breeds learn. You'll learn to vampire."

Gram kept her fangs in a glass by the sink. They looked distorted. They frightened me. I remember that glass by the sink cuz my teeth is starting to look just the same.

♦♦♦

**Sasha Janel McBrayer**'s short speculative fiction work has been published by *Silverthought Online, Wily Writers Speculative Fiction*, and *Title Goes Here*. Her arts and entertainment vblog, "Showtime with Sasha", is a weekly offering at coastalcourier.com. She lives in Savannah, GA and keeps a blog at nikanors-inn.livejournal.com.

# "The Tunnel"

## by Matt Cowens

Gregor slipped through the gap in the fence and into the open space of the park. He dashed forward and dive-rolled behind a steel climbing frame, then sprang up into a crouch. Nobody in sight.

He sized up the distance to the tunnel. The late afternoon sun had little warmth in it as it filtered down through the haze of concrete dust. Pulse cannons had been firing shells over the river for days now and Gregor's house, the whole neighbourhood, was coated in a fine grey mist. He wiped the back of his hand across his eyes and broke cover.

He ignored the distant thudding of mortars as he reached the tunnel, skidded into its dark concrete interior. It was an old bit of pipe from an early colony construction site, three feet in diameter and ten feet long. It had been dropped into a trench of cement so that it was fixed in place in the middle of the playground. It had proved as popular as the colourful steel climbing frame or the swings.

In the shadowy interior of the pipe Gregor leaned back against the curved surface, his knees by his head, and looked at the graffiti. The inside of the pipe was covered with swear words and rude jokes, stick figure colony soldiers fighting giant spiders, faded hearts filled with initials. There was more ink than blank concrete. He traced the outline of a heart with one finger. Did the initials inside belong to someone Gregor knew? Someone from his school?

Gregor reached into his pocket and pulled the marker out. He hesitated, then picked a clear space, reached up and drew an F. The black slashes went a little wonky on the curved surface of the tunnel. He took more care with the U. His additions to the cacophony of graffiti screamed out at him, obviously new, obviously clumsy. Others had written their names with jagged skill, or drawn hugely endowed men with guns as big as their erections killing spindly spiderkind. His writing was childish next to those accomplishments.

Gregor felt a hollow sickness in his stomach. The light was failing and his father would soon realise he was not home.

Blinking the hot sting of tears from his eyes, Gregor stabbed at the concrete with his marker, scrawled the rest of the word before stumbling out of the tunnel, through the park and back towards his house.

At dinner his parents were serious, their voices low. His father talked of spiderkind battalions and advances. His mother talked of children lost in the fighting, of colony ships diverted to safer worlds. Gregor couldn't follow most of it. He was too busy fretting over the marker.

He'd left it in the tunnel.

All his stationery was carefully labelled, his name scratched into every pencil, every pen. He'd been meticulous about it. And now some mother was going to take her child to the park, was going to hear the horrified screams as her child saw his profanity, would find the incriminating marker and tell his parents what he'd done.

Gregor did not sleep that night. He lay awake, listening to his parents arguing. He heard the clink of glass bottles as his father went out in spite of his mother's protests. He lay awake, knowing what he had to do but paralysed by fear. Would he be seen by soldiers, a dark shape moving through the city, and be challenged? Shot? Would he run into his father, delivering his crate of bottles with oily rags stuffed in their necks? Gregor squirmed as he imagined the look of bitter disappointment creasing his father's tired face as he realised his son had broken another one of his rules.

Gregor slipped from his bed and dressed as quietly as he could. Better to risk everything now than to wait. He opened his window, the sound of distant gunfire suddenly louder in the stillness of his room, and clambered out.

Gregor's feet barely touched the ground as he raced through the empty streets to the park, cutting through an alleyway and two back yards. The sound of fighting was further off than it had been that afternoon. Slipping from shadow to shadow he felt a flush of confidence, a thrill at being out under the stars. It was going to work. He could collect the marker and his parents would never know.

His heart sank as he reached the park and heard the rough voices of men, urgent and angry. He dared a quick glance through a gap in the fence and saw shapes close to him, moving in the darkness. Dust and clouds blocked the moon but he could make out the silhouettes of rifles, of pistols, the dim glow of cigarettes.

He sank to the ground, his back against the fence. Had it been for nothing? Would he fail now, having risked everything? He pictured himself slinking back home, trying to explain the dirt on his hands in the morning, his father opening the door to a young girl crying, her horrified mother clutching the marker in meaty fingers.

The clouds overhead slid past the moon and the park brightened. Suddenly exposed, Gregor scrambled and slipped behind a bin. As he did so he caught a glimpse of a glorious sight and his heart soared. One of the men stood atop a pile of broken concrete at the heart of a crater in the park. Smoke rose lazily from the remnants of the swing and the metal climbing frame was a twisted mass of broken steel. The angry voices grew clearer as Gregor saw what they were lamenting, the devastation of a mortar attack.

Gregor sighed and slumped back. The spiderkind must have advanced their pulse cannons. The war had crossed the river, had reached his neighbourhood.

Gregor smiled. Everything would be all right. The park had been destroyed.

◆ ◆ ◆

**Matt Cowens** lives and writes on the Kapiti Coast of New Zealand with his wife and son. He also teaches English and Media Studies, records the occasional podcast, and makes and appears in short films. He maintains a very infrequently updated blog at www.mattcowens.livejournal.com

# "Reckoning"

## by Bruce Golden

Two down, sacks loaded, three and one—I knew I had to throw a strike. I figured I could throw one by him. Nothing fancy...go with the heat...muscle-up and blow it by him.

Ruiz, my catcher, he gives me the sign for a yakker. I'm thinking he's crazy. No way I'm risking a breaking ball three and one. Anyway, I knew I could throw it by this guy. He was nothing. He was meat on a stick. So I shook off the sign.

He puts down three fingers for the change. I'm thinking screw him, I can blow this guy away. I shake him off again.

Finally he gives me the number-one, my bread and butter. I figure I'll throw it by him, then three and two and he's mine.

I windup, put a little extra juice on it, and let fly…

Next thing I know I'm listening to the P.A. guy.

"It's a graaand slaaam, folks. Rusty Storr's 13th homer of the season."

He slammed me. I couldn't believe it. How'd he catch up with that pitch?

I knew when I saw Maggio pop his ugly head out of the dugout and start my way I was screwed. I was in no mood to listen to his crap, but I knew that wasn't gonna stop him.

"What kind of pitch was that? You call that pitching? My grandmother could've thrown that fat one."

"Bring in your grandmother then."

"You're outta here. Give me the ball."

"It's all yours," I said, flipping it to him as I walked away.

"Hey! Get back here and wait for your relief."

I thought of several clever comebacks, but I kept them to myself. Maggio, though, wasn't gonna let it go that easy.

"Yeah, well just keep on going. You're washed-up anyway, yuh bum."

I flashed him the international symbol of disrespect and kept going.

It wasn't that I disagreed with his evaluation of my skills. I just didn't cotton to his managerial style.

Now it's funny the things you notice at a time like that. The first thing I focused on during that long walk back to the dugout was the moths dancing around the light towers. Then I saw the mascot trying to drink a beer he had begged off some fan. Most of it was dribbling down the front of his costume. And, though it was the last thing on my mind, my eyes fastened on to this annie with a chest like two softballs—the giant mushball kind they use in the Sunday beer leagues. But she wasn't paying any attention to me. She was checking out Donner at first base.

As casual as I tried to act, by the time I got to the bench I was ready to puke my guts out. It had become a familiar feeling. Six years in the minors and my arm wasn't getting any younger. I wasn't no poet laureate, but I could read the writing on the wall. In big, bright letters, it spelled LOSER.

♦

When I finally woke up my mouth felt like I'd been sucking on a resin bag. My head was ringing so loud I might as well as have been beaned by one of my own fastballs. I didn't want to open my eyes, but I knew I'd have to eventually. I thought back to try and figure out what had left me in this condition, and what I might find when I did risk a look. All I remembered was the big dinger I'd given up, and a lineup of empty shot glasses.

I took a peek and realized I wasn't alone. Had the pounding in my head not been so heavy, I probably would've noticed someone was lying on my arm. So I had no choice but to open my eyes and take a good look.

God, she was an ugly one. I mean, don't get me wrong, she had a great body, if you like the pillowy look, but her face belonged in a manual explaining why catchers wear masks. It wasn't the first time I'd woken up next to a bowser, and I figured it probably wouldn't be the last, but this one was going for the record. To get away without waking her, I would've chewed my arm off right then and there, but it was my pitching arm, and there was at least a slim chance I might still need it. Fortunately, it wasn't long before she rolled over, freeing me to get the hell out of Dodge.

Once outside I found myself in some part of town I didn't recognize. I started walking, hoping I'd find a taxi or something. By then it was all coming back to me, and I'm wishing I was still asleep. It didn't take much remembering to recall my pitching career was on the fast-track to Nowheresville, and last night I'd punched my own ticket. I knew I'd be lucky to last the season. At my age, they wouldn't even bother sending me down. It would be *c'est la vie* and *sayonara*—thanks for the memories. I had to face facts. I was never even gonna get a cup of coffee in the bigs.

It was still early, a Sunday morning I think. There wasn't even nobody on the street for me to ask where the hell I was. Then I heard this *guh-thump* noise. Then again, *guh-thump...guh-thump.* I figure whoever's making the racket can tell me how to get back to the ballpark, but when I turn the corner I see it's some kid, maybe ten or eleven. He's got his cap on ass-backwards like the kids do today, his pointy little ears sticking up like flags, and he's throwing a ball against this cement wall...*guh-thump...guh-thump.* He's trying to pitch, but his follow-through has all the grace of a drunken giraffe. Speaking of which, by now I'm close enough that the *guh-thump* is echoing inside my hangover.

*Guh-thump.*

"Hey, whatcha doing?" I yell to him.

*Guh-thump.*

"Practicing," he answers without stopping.

*Guh-thump.*

Then, 'cause I can't take any more *guh-thumps,* I grab the ball on the rebound before he can glove it.

"You'll never throw strikes like that, kid. You gotta bring your arm over the top like this, and follow-through across your body after you release it."

"How would you know?" he says real smartass like.

"Cause I'm a pitcher, kid. Here, try it like this."

I wound up and let one go, easy-like. It hit dead-center inside the chalked circle the kid had drawn on the wall. I saw he was impressed, so I worked with his form for a few minutes, just so I'd smoothed it out enough that he wasn't practicing any more bad habits. He was a quick learner.

"Try one more."

The kid wound up and fired...dead center, right down the heart.

"There, just like magic."

He gave me a quick smile, retrieved his ball, and shot me one of those glances kids do when they've got a serious question.

"You believe in magic?"

"Me? I believe if you work your butt off you might, just might, be lucky enough to make it. But if you don't, all the magic in the world won't do you no good. That's what your pitching needs now—lots of work. Just keep practicing until you can throw nine out of ten inside your target."

"Nine out of ten?" he repeated as if I'd asked him to memorize the Bill of Rights.

"Hey, if you want to be the best, you gotta be willing to pay the price."

"The price?"

"Yeah, whatever it takes. Everything's got a price. You gotta sacrifice. You gotta give to get. There's always a reckoning. Didn't anybody ever teach you that?"

"Are you the best?"

"Yeah...right. Hell, I'd give anything to be the best—even for a day."

Then he says to me, real grownup-like, "I guess you didn't sacrifice enough, huh?"

He froze me for a second with that, like a southpaw with a real good pick-off move.

"Hell, you're a kid, what do you know?"

He just flashed me this big grin.

"Now, tell me how I get out of here. Point me in the direction of the ballpark, kid."

He grabbed my arm and pointed down the street. As soon as he touched me I felt this electric tingle, kinda like when you smack your funny bone and things go numb for a second. It ran from my fingers all the way up through my shoulder.

"You can go that way there," he said, "or you can take the short cut."

"Give me the short cut, kid, I'm in a hurry."

♦

My next start I pitched a one-hitter. I followed that with a no-hitter—yeah, no bull. My arm felt like it was 19 again. I can't explain it—it just came out of nowhere. All of a sudden I'm hitting my spots, my curveball's breaking like a mother-trucker, and my heater's in the mid-nineties. I mean I'm throwing some serious gas.

About the same time the big club got a little desperate. They were in a pennant race and one of their starters went down with a bad wing. So they looked around and there I was. They gambled and jumped me from Double-A all the way to the majors. That's how I finally made it to the Show.

I get my first start against the Cards, and I'm one nervous rookie. I'm standing there on the lip of the dugout, soaking it all up. The stands full of people, the scoreboard with my name in the starting lineup, my teammates getting pumped for the first pitch, and I'm thinking this is the same field where Musial played...the same mound where Gibson pitched. Swear-to-God, I'm standing there tingling all over, when I see the kid. The same kid I was showing how to pitch a couple weeks back. Only that was on the other side of the country. But I'm sure it's him—same hat on ass-backwards, same pointy ears. I stare at him, but he's just sitting there in the stands, field level.

Number 16 pats me on the behind on his way to take the field and I snap out of it. I decide to figure out the kid later, 'cause I got a game to pitch.

♦

Despite a case of the shakes that has me walking the leadoff man on four straight, everything's still working and I pitch my way out of some trouble. I'm holding them scoreless through eight, and getting ready to go out for the ninth with a two-nothing lead. The guys are slapping me on the back, telling me to close it out, and I happen to look over to the stands. What do I see but that damn kid again. This time he looks right at me and flashes that little grin of his. I'm still trying to figure out how he might've got there, when it's time to take the mound.

I strike out the first guy, but then I give up a bloop single. While I'm worrying about the guy on first, the next batter drives one into the gap. Now I really got something to worry about. It's second and third and I can see them scurrying around in the pen. I decide to go from the windup, but fall behind three and one. The catcher calls for Uncle Charlie and I shake him off. Then he puts down three fingers, but I want to come with the heat, so I shake him off again.

Strike two. Strike three.

I blow the guy away with a couple of pills. Now I just need one more out for the win. I come with another fastball and crack! Suddenly a line shot's coming right at my head. I swipe at it with my glove as I'm falling to get the hell out of the way. It hits me somewhere and I hit the ground. The next thing I know, the crowd is dead silent and my teammates are pulling me up.

Talk about luck. The ball was jammed into the webbing of my glove. The game was over and I had my first major league win. On my way off the field, I'm high-fiving, low-fiving, and then I remember the kid and look over to where he was sitting, but he's not there anymore. At this point, I don't really care, 'cause I got a W.

♦

I didn't stop there, no sir. I threw a one-hit shutout at Cincinnati my second start, then a five-hitter against the Cubs at Wrigley. Before you know it, I'm getting more press in the clubhouse than an ironing board. Oh yeah, they also signed me to a three-year major league contract—big bucks. If I told you how many zeros you wouldn't believe me.

Not long after that I met Sonja, the kind of classy woman I never figured would go for me. In less time than it takes to play a four-game series, we fell in lust, in love, got crazy, and got married. Then, believe it or not, the day after our 48-hour honeymoon, I no-hit the Giants. Was I living a charmed life or what?

I didn't stop to worry about how long it would last, I rode that puppy for all it was worth. I rode it all the way into the last game of the season. A win would put us into the playoffs and I drew the start.

In the clubhouse before the game, the guys are all pretty loose. Someone's got ESPN on the tube, and I'm trying to look like I'm not listening, even though I am, 'cause the guy's talking about me.

"...of course he hasn't proven it over the course of a whole season."

"That's right, Dan. No one knows if he's just fooling hitters because they haven't seen his stuff enough, or if he's the real thing. But right now, he's the best pitcher in baseball."

"That would be tough to argue with. As for the rest of the staff...."

◆

It was a tough game. I threw the hell out of the ball, but these guys were no pushovers. By the top of the ninth it was 3-3, and I was just about out of gas. On my way out to the mound something catches my eye, and I glance into the stands. It's funny in that sea of faces I would spot him—looked right at him and didn't even notice anyone else. It was the kid again. Different city, same kid. He kind of waved to me with this serious but dopey look on his face. Not knowing what else to do, I nodded to him and took the mound. While I'm warming up, I get curious and look back at the kid, or at least where he was. Now I can't see him.

Anyway, I got two quick outs, but the next guy plays pepper with the outfield wall and my leftfielder kicks it around. So I've got the go-ahead run on third and the way they're heating up in the pen, I know this is my last batter. Which is just as well, 'cause my arm is dead anyway. I start him with a curve and then come in with the change. He's oh-and-two before he knows it, and hasn't a clue what to look for. I decide to throw a B-B on the outside corner. I windup, let fly, and crack! Only it's not the sound of the ball hitting the bat, 'cause I just whiffed the guy. I've got enough time to see him swing and miss before the pain knocks me to the ground. That's when I see my pitching arm, dangling like a piece of cooked spaghetti.

♦

If you follow the game, you probably know I never pitched again. But I did see that kid once more. It's crazy, but I'm sure it was the same kid. It was eight or nine years later, long after the cancer had gotten so bad that they had to amputate.

I was sitting there, watching Sam play. Yeah, Sonja had stuck with me, and we had a little boy. Well I'm watching him play ball—he's out at shortstop and he makes this great stab and throw on a grounder in the hole. I'm talking major league play here. So all the parents are clapping and whistling as the team runs in, and that's when this kid comes up to me. I don't recognize him at first. Why should I? The kid I remembered should've been full-grown by now. But this kid holds out a baseball card, and I see it's mine—the only one they ever made of me.

"Could you sign this for me?" he asks real polite like.

Now you gotta know I don't get that many requests. I was such a flash-in-the-pan, not many even remember me, especially a kid like this, who should've been in diapers when I made the bigs. So he's catching me off guard, but I take the card from him.

"Sure, kid," I say, using the pen he hands me.

"It's too bad about your arm," he says right out, which surprises me again, 'cause most people are afraid to even mention it.

"Yeah, life's tough."

"But you were the best once, weren't you?"

I finish signing the card, look up to hand it back, and that's when I recognize him. It's the same kid I stumbled on that day I was lost—the same kid. I knew it was him, but I also knew it couldn't be, 'cause this kid looked exactly the same. I mean he hadn't aged an inning.

"Yeah, kid. I guess I was the best...for a time."

He takes the card, glances at the signature, and looks back up at me, with his cap still on ass-backwards, his ears pointing up at the sky, and asks, "Was it worth it?"

I knew right away where he was coming from.

"Sure was, kid. Hell yes."

Novelist, journalist, satirist—**Bruce Golden**'s short stories have been published more than 90 times across eight countries. *Asimov's Science Fiction* described his second novel, "If Mickey Spillane had collaborated with both Frederik Pohl and Philip K. Dick, he might have produced Bruce Golden's *Better Than Chocolate*," and said about his novel, *Evergreen*, "If you can imagine Ursula Le Guin channeling H. Rider Haggard, you'll have the barest conception of this stirring book, which centers around a mysterious artifact and the people in its thrall." You can read more of Golden's stories in his recently published collection *Dancing with the Velvet Lizard*.

goldentales.tripod.com

# "Stuff of the Elder Gods"

## by K.C. Ball

Kerry Egan twitched as the plate-glass door slapped shut behind her. Outside the diner, the November winds howled off the flats along the river, demanding her return.

Ivy Duncan, Kerry's co-worker, stood at the register. Two men hunched over the counter, one near Ivy, the other at the far end. Ivy's face looked whiter than her uniform. Neither of the men turned when the door slammed. No sign of Eddie Becker, either, although his West Virginia State Police cruiser sat in the parking lot.

*Something has gone wrong here.*

"Help you, Ma'am?" Ivy asked.

*Ma'am?*

Ivy's head never moved but her eyes turned toward the end of the counter. Kerry risked a look and spotted gleaming black uniform boots, toes up, on the floor. Brand-new Rockies, like the pair Eddie showed her yesterday.

One of Kerry's notions had come that morning. Nana Comer used to call them second sight. Bundled in her bed, snug against the cold, reading that new book of old poetry, Kerry heard a whisper. *Stay home today.*

She should have listened. For one sick instant, she wanted to go look at those boots. No. *Better drive away and call 911. Play it smart.* "How far is Moundsville?"

"Just down the road a piece." Ivy pointed south. "You can't miss it."

"Thanks." As Kerry turned to go, someone racked a shotgun.

"Lock that door and get your ass on in here," one of the strangers said.

Kerry locked the door and turned around.

The man at the end of the counter had the sixteen-gauge. Tall and thin and marked, a beanpole with forearms covered by tattoos, like the ones Kerry's daddy sported when he came home from the correctional up to Wheeling. The man grinned. "We ain't stupid. You got waitress scrawled all over you."

The second man, a runt, had a round face with a scruffy beard. He gestured with a nasty-looking pistol. "Give me the coat and purse."

Kerry did as he said. The man tossed the coat aside, after checking the pockets, then upended her purse onto the counter. He pawed through her things until he touched her keys. He scooped them up, dangling the silver pig medallion. "What the hell is this?"

♦

Kerry thought the same thing when she spotted the medallion at a used book store in Parkersburg, the same place she found the dog-eared copy of William Butler Yeats' *The Wind Among the Reeds*. Both sparked dreams of long-gone times. She didn't blink when the clerk told her how much. Some things you had to have.

The medallion had heft and size, big as a quarter. An etching of a wild boar, with tusks and razored back, marked both faces. Kerry figured the thing to be pure silver, but couldn't figure out if it might be artifact or knockoff.

The book proved just as curious. The publisher's page had been ripped away, so she had no way to tell its age, but Kerry suspected it might be first edition.

The poems within sung to her. Yeats' passion for stuff of Celtic legends set Kerry to dreaming of another age, just as Nana Comer's stories did, once upon a time. Nana had been born in Ireland. A natural storyteller, she could spin the old tales. Doings of the gods, heroic battles with monsters, loves found and lost. Kerry never got enough.

"You've the stuff of the elder gods about you, child," Nana used to say.

Kerry's memories of winter nights seemed as vivid as if written on her mind just yesterday. Huddled at the farmhouse fireplace, swathed in quilts while the winds whistled across the chimney lip, munching popcorn, she had listened to Nana tell all those old stories.

♦

The runt still held her keys. "What's this?"

"A Celtic fertility charm."

"What?"

"It's for sex, you dumb shit," the beanpole said. "So you can get it up."

"Ain't never had that problem, Wayne. Have you?"

"Asshole."

The runt snatched up the Yeats. "Look here, Wayne. She reads poems, just like you."

"Shut up, Quincy."

Quincy mimicked Wayne. "*Shut up, Quincy.* I swear...I hear that one more time, I'll puke."

"Shut up, Quincy."

Quincy showed Wayne his middle finger. "We get away; you're on your own."

"Suits me."

Kerry turned to Ivy. "Who are these clowns?"

"They escaped the pen up in Wheeling." Ivy sounded like she'd had enough of this nonsense. "Came in here to snatch a car. The pipsqueak shot—"

"Shut up, old woman."

Ivy stepped toward Quincy, shook her finger in his face. "Listen here—"

Quincy grabbed her finger and twisted. The crisp snap of breaking bone filled the diner. Ivy wailed, slumped against the counter.

Something stirred within Kerry, something furious and ancient. "You bastard. I'll—"

Quincy pulled Ivy closer, pushed the barrel of his gun against her cheek. He peered at Kerry. "You'll what? Shut up, 'less you want to see her dead."

He twisted again and Ivy sobbed. Quincy let go of her finger. Kerry expected to see her friend collapse, but Ivy reached beneath the counter, came up with the Louisville Slugger she kept there.

She lurched toward Quincy. "I'll teach you some manners."

Quincy threw his free arm up just as she swung. The bat connected with the thick of his shoulder; he grunted with the blow. Ivy pulled back for another go and Quincy pulled the pistol into line.

Kerry grabbed at his collar, but the shirt ripped free with a stuttering stitch. The wild thing inside her shrieked. She clawed at Quincy's back.

Too late. The pistol cracked twice and Ivy's eyes dulled. She thumped against the wall, slid to the floor, leaving a bloody trail behind.

Quincy spun, trained the handgun on Kerry's face. "I'll do you, too, you bitch. Don't think I won't."

Kerry backed down but didn't look away. "I get the chance, you'll pay for that."

Quincy threw the keys at her. "Big talk don't win nothing. Take your shit and get behind the counter."

Kerry clutched the medallion, whispering words she wondered where or when she'd learned. Heat spiraled up her arm.

Quincy poked the gun at her again. "I *said*, get behind the counter."

Kerry got. She dropped her purse beneath the register and pushed the keys deep into her apron pocket. They settled against her belly, weighted and still very warm.

Quincy went back to his stool. "Here's how it's going to go. We're gonna sit here until dark—"

Outside, air brakes hissed and a diesel engine powered down. A truck door slammed and boot heels clocked across the asphalt. Inside, the three of them turned to the door.

"Shit, Wayne. She never locked up."

"Yes, she did. I watched her."

Quincy turned back on Kerry. "Cover up the old woman and come close where I can see you."

Kerry skirted Ivy's body, dropped her coat in place as she passed. No real concealment. Quincy and Wayne settled down and tried to hide their weapons.

"Don't you dare do nothing funny," Quincy said.

The door swung open and the wind rushed in with the driver, carrying the scent of coal dust and cold, brown river water.

"Glad you're open." The driver sounded like the actor who played the new James Bond. "Couldn't tell, outside, if you were here."

The driver dressed in faded jeans, expensive cowboy boots and a denim jacket, wore a Looney Tunes baseball cap with Porky Pig winking from the bull's eye.

He glanced toward Wayne and then settled on a stool just out of Quincy's reach. He thumbed back his cap and smiled at Kerry. "I don't suppose there's hope of getting bangers and mash with a cup of Earl Grey?"

"We might have tea bags in the back."

Quincy glared at Kerry over his coffee mug, but didn't say a word.

"Never mind," the driver said. "I'll settle for coffee."

"Do you want milk with that?"

"No. Just sugar."

Kerry filled a mug from one of the two glass carafes on the hotplate behind her. She set the mug before the driver, napkin-wrapped flatware, too. Her hands quivered as she worked.

"Ain't from around here, are you?" Wayne said.

The driver shook his head. "This is my first time in West Virginia, but I could get used to it. It smells like home."

He scooped up a dispenser, drizzled sugar into his coffee, then undid the napkin, took up the spoon and stirred.

Wayne made no effort to conceal the shotgun butt tucked into his armpit. The driver didn't seem to notice it. Didn't seem to see Quincy's torn shirt and bloody back. Didn't even ask why Ivy's coat-draped body lay behind the counter.

Instead, he sat, sipping his coffee.

Quincy shattered the silence. "What's in the trailer?"

"Pigs."

The driver winked at Kerry. Her heart struck a double beat and the silver medallion tucked against her belly flared once more with heat. She *knew* this man.

"It will be all right, wait and see," he said, and laid his hand atop hers to still the quiver.

"Hey, don't touch her." Wayne jumped to his feet.

Time slowed. Kerry could hear each click of the sweep hand on the wall clock, every sensation needle-sharp, the smell of deep-fryer fat, the coppered scent of blood, the beating of their four hearts, and the pigs grunting in the truck outside.

One of her notions came. *His name is Moccus.*

Moccus let go her hand. Time jerked into gear again. He plucked up the butter knife, sent the clumsy weapon tumbling. As it flew toward Wayne the blade changed, stretched and narrowed into a stiletto. Kerry blinked. When she looked again, the knife sprouted from the ruin of Wayne's left eye. He toppled from the stool. As he fell, the shotgun roared.

The blast caught Moccus in the chest.

"Sons-a-bitches," Kerry screamed.

Moving with what felt like super-human swiftness, she grabbed a carafe from the hot plate. The bastards would pay for all of this. But when she turned back, Moccus stood across the counter, clutching Quincy's throat. The little man babbled, as he wormed the pistol into place and fired three shots into Moccus' neck. Blood sprayed upon the tiles and tables.

"Oh, you bastard!" Kerry lunged across the counter and smashed the coffee-filled carafe against Quincy's head.

He screamed and dropped the pistol, pawing at his scalp and face. Kerry scrambled after him, but slipped on blood and coffee-wetted glass. Something crackled in her back as she hit the floor. No time to whimper, though. Quincy had gone to his knees to grope for his lost gun.

Kerry wobbled to her feet, skated to the door. Outside, she made it to her Jetta, then a gunshot cracked. The sheet metal dimpled next to Kerry's knee.

Quincy stood behind her. "Don't you dare try to get away from me."

A myriad of tiny cuts etched his bare torso and his face. Blood beaded on his cheeks and dripped from his chin. Most of his left ear had vanished and he pressed his left arm tight to his side.

But his pistol never wavered.

Something Kerry had forgotten exploded into life within her soul, something Quincy wasn't going to like. Old, deep-seated memories welled up, faster and faster.

Quincy limped toward her. "Just me and you now, in that little bitty car of yours."

"Be still."

"What did you say?"

He poked her belly with the pistol. Kerry thrust out one hand and the gun crumbled into dust.

Quincy stared at his empty hand. When he spoke his voice sounded as if he was breathing helium. "How'd you do that?"

She sighed. The man had become nothing but irksome shadow, her recollections more real to her just now. She'd run from a lovers' spat, assumed false memories to become Kerry. "I was—"

Quincy slapped her cheek with his bloody hand. She thrust out her hand again and waved him away. He tumbled across the asphalt, as if blown by fearsome winds, scrambled to his feet and wobbled north toward the Ohio River.

Kerry watched him run, just as she had run, and she saw the truth of it. Even a goddess can be trapped by careless magic. Time to tidy up her mess.

She raised her hand a third time. The rear doors of the pig hauler opened and a ramp slid from a hidden channel. Bright eyes peered from the darkness. Kerry's fingers curled and a drift of pigs descended. Droop-eared Landraces. They came to her, bright-eyed and expectant. She strolled among them, tweaking ears, scratching shoulders, cooing to her pets. "Bring him to me."

The pigs moved as one to do her bidding.

"Hello, Cerridwen."

Kerry turned toward the voice. Moccus stood not far away, looking none the worse for the struggle in the diner.

Kerry smiled. "Hello, my love."

Moccus came to her. As he touched her, the heat returned and even memory of the pain left her, as if water draining from an open standpipe.

"Is this your doing?" she asked.

Moccus shook his head. "Only the medallion and the book. I'm sorry about your friends."

"So am I. I like the book, though. It was a nice touch."

Moccus drew the Yeats' book from nothingness and struck a pose. "Away, come away; empty your heart of its mortal dream. The winds awaken, the leaves whirl round. Our cheeks are pale, our hair unbound."

"The old romantic had a way with words, didn't he?"

"A clever fellow. I always liked him."

The pigs drew near again. One of them had a chunk of ear missing. The diner door slammed twice, another Landrace snuffled into view. Lean and disfigured, missing its left eye. It joined the others as they climbed into the trailer. Wayne and Quincy would be traveling together, after all.

Kerry gestured and the ramp slid in place, the doors swung shut. She glanced south along the highway. The faint wail of approaching sirens floated on the winds.

Moccus tipped his head toward his truck. "Shall we go?"

Kerry waved away the question. "I can't leave just yet. Ivy deserves a proper send-off."

Moccus considered the truck for a beat, glanced back to the south. "All right."

Shoulders touching, fingers entwined, they waited. The winds, no longer quite so cold, ruffled Kerry's clothing and her russet hair. The lights floated nearer, hard along the highway.

Moccus drew his shoulders back. "Ready?"

"As I ever was."

"I'll play the handsome stranger," he said.

"I be the plucky miner's daughter," she replied.

"I arrived after you escaped and the outlaws got away."

"As you say."

The first of the police cars slewed into the parking lot, siren wailing like a forlorn banshee. Loose gravel fanned away from its tires.

Kerry leaned close to Moccus, whispering. "The constables don't need to know those two got their comeuppance."

Moccus nodded. "Punishment to fit the deed. Yeats would have loved it."

Kerry nodded. "You're right. He always had a soft spot for stuff of the elder gods."

**K.C. Ball** lives in Seattle. In addition to *Wily Writers*, her short fiction has appeared in print and online in such publications as *Analog, Lightspeed, Flash Fiction Online* and *Murky Depths*. K.C. won the *L. Ron Hubbard Writers of the Future* award in 2009. She is a 2010 graduate of the Clarion West writers workshop and an active member of the Science Fiction and Fantasy Writers of America. Her short story collection, *Snapshots from a Black Hole & Other Oddities*, is available from Hydra House Books.

# "Timeshare"

by Fred Warren

They time-shared me to Chuckie Lee Wilson after he died. If you take a life, you give your life. That's the law now. No excuses, no shades of gray.

Chuckie Lee car-jacked me at a dark intersection downtown. When he broke through my window, I stepped on the gas and dragged him for three blocks. The prosecutors told me I was lucky the upload crew got to him in time, or I would have spent the rest of my life in a cage.

"He was going to kill me," I said.

"Nobody knows what he planned to do," they said. "Chuckie Lee Wilson is dead, and you killed him."

"I didn't mean to kill him. He had a gun, and I panicked. His sleeve caught on the door."

"You could have stopped the car. Instead, you took his life. Now you're going to give it back."

So, Chuckie Lee gets half my life in exchange for the life I took from him. Monday, Wednesday, and Friday are mine. Tuesday, Thursday, and Saturday are his. We trade off on Sundays. I wear a tracker locked onto my ankle.

Monday night, I ride the bus to Chuckie Lee's apartment on the East Side. The state pays his rent and sends him an allowance so he doesn't have to work. I clip on the wires from the upload box, lie on his bed, and press the button. It's like getting hit in the head with a jagged rock. I go into the box, and Chuckie Lee goes into my brain. Inside the box, there's nothing. I sleep, but I don't dream.

Tuesday belongs to Chuckie Lee.

Wednesday morning, I wake up and deal with whatever Chuckie Lee did to my body the day before. I'm hung-over. My mouth tastes like road kill, and my clothes stink of cigarettes and weed. My face and hands are bruised and cut. I shower and take the bus to work. Anybody who talks to me stops when they notice the tracker.

I'm no good at my job anymore. I forget things. My company wants to fire me, but the court won't let them. The judge says it would have an adverse impact on Chuckie Lee. After work, I order take-out and eat it at home in front of the TV. Then I go back to Chuckie Lee's, and it starts all over again—Thursday, Friday, Saturday, and every other Sunday.

On my Sunday, there's no upload that night, and I sleep in my own bed. I dream, but I don't want to. I see Chuckie Lee's face, pleading, twisted in agony. I hear him scream as the pavement tears him apart, over and over again.

I used to be married. Melanie was pretty, and we were happy together until I killed Chuckie Lee. When the time-share started, Melanie couldn't handle it, knowing Chuckie Lee was inside my head. She was scared to be alone with me. Chuckie Lee came after her one Tuesday, and she fought him off with a kitchen knife. Friday morning, Melanie was gone. I think she went back to live with her folks. I don't remember. I wear long sleeves to hide the scars.

I wonder sometimes what it's like for Chuckie Lee. I left him a note once: "Please take better care of my body. You got a second chance. Do something good with your life." He didn't reply. The hangovers just got worse. His friends sit on the apartment steps and laugh at me when I go inside to do the upload. "How's it feel to be Chuckie Lee's ride, Slick? Serves you right."

I passed another time-share on the street last week. His clothes were torn and dirty, and he staggered as he walked. He was a teenager, but his hands shook like an old man's. When he saw the tracker, he stared at me like he was drowning, like I was the only person in the world who could understand, begging me to save him.

I turned away. Save him? I couldn't save myself.

I want my life back, the part they stole from me and gave to Chuckie Lee, the part he beats up, and poisons, and wastes, one day at a time. I want to drive my car again and have dreams that aren't nightmares. I want Melanie. I want to remember.

I'm tired of sharing.

♦♦♦

**Fred Warren**'s short fiction has appeared in a variety of print and online publications including *Kaleidotrope, Every Day Fiction, Bards & Sages Quarterly, Allegory*, and, of course, *Wily Writers*. His first novel, *The Muse*, debuted in November 2009 from Splashdown Books, and his short-story anthology, *Odd Little Miracles*, was published in July, 2011. Fred works as a government contractor in eastern Kansas, where he lives with his wife and three children. You can find him online at frederation.wordpress.com.

# "A Necessity of the Present"

by Jeremy Zimmerman

Inspector Tenuk and his men could hear the pounding drums and shrill pipes from outside the warehouse. The aged wooden planks that framed the structure did nothing to contain the wall of noise that rolled out. The tribes who left their forests and mountains behind to live in the city brought their music with them. The wild rhythm drew in the younger residents of Haven, gathering them together in the remote sections of the city for their so-called "revels." There they danced with reckless abandon, imbibed illicit substances, and rutted like animals. The revelers claimed they embraced life in its simplest, rawest form. Others thought the kids just did it to piss off their parents.

The inspector hid in the shadow of a tenement building. The tattered clothing he bundled himself in gave him the appearance of a vagrant. The soot and dirt spread over his scales added to that image and muted his skin's scarlet sheen. In neighboring buildings, other constables also lurked in disguise.

The revel on its own did not bring Inspector Tenuk to this sparsely populated part of town. Instead, Tenuk waited patiently from his viewpoint for a goblin pimp named Silky. The Empire had licensed brothels, but some vices fell outside of even those generous boundaries. These forbidden fruits resulted in a business opportunity for creatures like Silky. The revels had a tendency to attract the darker aspects of the city, and Silky in particular liked to come there and recruit young people who were too wasted to understand what they were getting themselves into.

The constables had been there for hours. Tenuk's forked tongue darted between his lips occasionally, tasting the air. Even from across the street, the air reeked with the musky smell of sweat and sex, the spicy scent of opium and qat, and the sharp acidic tang of vomit and urine.

An anxious note entered the reckless sounds rolling across the street, a tremulous murmur that slowly ate away at the joyous noise. The music faltered, screams of terror swelled. Soon revelers poured out of the warehouse, stepping on one another in their efforts to escape the building.

The inspector signaled his men and went wading in through the mob. He and his fellow constables formed a disciplined wedge driving through the waves of terrified youths, stepping over the crushed bodies of fallen revelers. Five years prior someone had summoned a demon at a revel because they thought it would be "fun," and Tenuk had lost a lot of men beating that thing back into the abyss. If this was a repeat, it was best that they act fast.

By the time they got inside, most of the revelers were gone. What few remained were too injured, stunned, or drugged to flee. Tenuk's eyes quickly landed on the source of all the terror. He and his men slowly approached the prone form sprawled out on the bare earth floor.

The young man lying face down in the dirt looked like an angel, even though Tenuk knew that this was not the case. Pale skin, golden hair, fashionably clad in expensive clothes thrown on with little care. Wings came out of the young man's back through his specially tailored clothing, the downy white feathers contrasting sharply with the blood they soaked in. From beneath the young man's body a pool of red slowly spread out over the dirt, seeping out from a wound concealed from view. The smell of flowers filled the air around the body.

Tenuk took a deep breath and slowly released it as he cursed, "Shit."

♦

The sun rose up over the city as Sir Donaliel approached the warehouse. Agents of the constabulary swarmed over the area: guards keeping the curious away, sketch artists recording every detail they could, forensic thaumaturges huddled together in some sort of discussion. Bunches of flowers were arranged nearby, as people began to mark the passing of a royal.

The crowd did not hinder Sir Donaliel at all. Bystanders parted before him as they stared in mute awe. Even with more open borders and trade between neighboring realms, the fae were still not a common presence in the city.

The knight flashed his Imperial writ at one of the guards as he lifted his long legs over the rope barrier. Inside the warehouse incense burned as more thaumaturges chanted to bring out any latent evidence that might help with the case. The knight pursed his lips in disgust at the dried signs of blood, vomit, and other bodily fluids soaked into the hard packed dirt. Sir Donaliel was able to quickly identify the responding officer, Inspector Tenuk, talking with some other constables in low tones. Most of the constables on duty were human, with goblins, trolls, and gnomes mixed in.

Tenuk was the only drakin. His red scales and fanged maw stood in sharp contrast to his peers.

A chalk outline next to the cluster of constables indicated where Prince Aleatoire's body had been, the ground bleached white where the prince's blood had spilled. Imperial princes had died in the past, but never so ignobly.

The constables looked up as Sir Donaliel approached. None offered any greeting.

"Good morning," the knight said. "Sir Donaliel of the Sun Guard, here on behalf of His Imperial Majesty to investigate the death of his son. You must be Inspector Tenuk."

"Must be," the drakin grunted.

"Is the investigation proceeding well?" Sir Donaliel continued, not allowing the curt tone to ruffle him.

"It'll all be in the report," the inspector mumbled, indicating that he was done with the conversation by beginning to turn away.

"Inspector," the knight said sharply to regain Tenuk's attention. "I realize that there exists a certain obligatory animosity from the constabulary towards the higher ranking organizations in the Empire." Tenuk's orange eyes narrowed at the use of the phrase "higher ranking organizations," but Sir Donaliel did not let it slow him as he continued. "And I understand that there is often resentment when other agencies take a case out from under the constables. But let me assure you that in this situation we recognize that the constabulary is better suited to carry it out. Murder is not something the Sun Guard is well suited to investigate. I am only here to represent the will of the Imperial Crown, not take your work away from you."

"Well," Tenuk said dryly, "My concerns are dispelled. At least I don't have one of the Moon Watch here instead, or else I might have a dagger in my ribs."

An awkward silence settled between them as both regarded the other quietly. Sir Donaliel finally broke the dead air that hung there.

"What have you discovered?"

"Looks pretty cut and dry," Tenuk said with a shrug. "Well, as cut and dry as something like this can be at least. Prince Al was stabbed with a special dagger." The knight felt his eye twitch at the familiar term used for the prince. "Thaumaturges tell me it was raw Chaos tempered in the flames of Hell, called it a..."

"Fellblade," Sir Donaliel stated flatly.

"You've heard of it?" Tenuk said with faint surprise.

"There are not many ways to kill a nephilim like Prince Aleatoire," the fae answered. "As a protector of the Imperial family, I am familiar with all possible avenues of threat. As you were saying?"

"Shame Prince Al didn't benefit from that protection," the inspector jibed. "But I guess being the youngest and least important member of the Imperial family must not have gotten you a whole lot of resources allocated to keep your celestial ass safe."

Sir Donaliel stiffened. "You come very close to treason."

"Prince Al was down here most nights of the week, looking for new things to fuck and new ways to destroy his brain," Tenuk countered. Wisps of smoke drifted from the inspector's nostrils. "We'd raid the particularly bad revels, inevitably picking up the prince in our sweep. He wouldn't even bother running. The guy knew he had a get out of jail free card and he wasn't interested in the effort it took to run. The only time we saw any of your 'Loyal and Honorable Knights of the Sun,'" Sir Donaliel did not miss Tenuk's use of the formal term for the Sun Guard in a derisive manner, "was when they came by for the customary escort out of jail. We can spend the rest of the day dancing around in circles and inflating the glorious memory of dear old Prince Al, or we can call a spade a spade and get on with our jobs. Do you want to catch the person who did this or do you want me to kiss your ass?"

The knight glared at Tenuk for several seconds before spitting out, "Fine. You were saying."

"Right, so he was stabbed with a fellblade. The alchemists haven't gotten to run any tests, but I'm expecting he had some cocktail going through his veins that slowed his reactions. Either that or the killer was just crazy good. If we catch the person who did this, I'm really hoping Al's reactions were slowed. The wound so far doesn't look like it was initially lethal, but the fellblade caused the prince's divine flesh near the wound to necrotize rapidly. It probably spread to his heart and that's what killed him. Falling on the dagger and shoving it farther in was just gravy."

"Any leads?" Sir Donaliel asked impatiently.

"Nah, we ain't got shit," the inspector said with a shrug. "We've spent all morning questioning what few brain dead hooligans hadn't managed to run off to whatever hole they hide in. For all that we got a lot of blank looks and a few tears from people who somehow gave a shit about the asshole." In response to a look from the fae, Tenuk added, "Or His Royal Assholeness if you want to be formal."

"What do you plan on doing next?" the knight pushed.

"I've been up all night wearing clothes that make my scales itch, and things went downhill from there" Inspector Tenuk answered. "I'm going to get cleaned up, change out of these rags, and get a bite to eat. Then, because you will otherwise get your gonads all up in a wad if I delay any further, I'm going to start asking some questions."

♦

"YUUUH-MEEZ!" the troll bellowed out over the heads of the shoppers in the market place. "YUUUH-MEEZ!"

The inspector led Sir Donaliel through the late morning crowds, making his way to the troll's stand. The transaction was wordless. Tenuk held up three fingers, the troll pulled three skewers out of the brazier with the burnt remains of some sort of large lizard on the end, and Tenuk gave the troll a handful of coins in exchange for the lizard.

"What on earth is that?" the knight asked with disgust apparent in his voice.

"Breakfast," Tenuk said enthusiastically before biting the head off of one of the lizards. Blood and grease poured out of the lizard. Despite being heavily charred on the outside, the innards were still mostly raw. The drakin allowed himself a satisfied smile as Sir Donaliel seemed to turn pale up to the pointy tips of his ears.

"So, um, what is your plan?" the fae asked, his gaze aimed pointedly away from the inspector.

"Not many places you can get something 'forged in the fires of Hell,'" Tenuk said through a mouthful of lizard. He began leading the way through the crowd again. "Couple people I know to ask, assuming it was procured locally. If it wasn't, then I just need to start kicking in doors and improvising."

"I have a feeling it is a local suspect," the knight commented, lagging a bit behind the inspector as they waded through the crowds of the marketplace.

"How so?" the inspector asked. A bit of motion from an alley caught Tenuk's eye. He'd seen someone following them since he left his apartments, but he was trying not to show his hand.

"While I lack your connections and experience with murder, the Sun Guard does occasionally deal with the criminal element. Not to mention political intrigue," Sir Donaliel commented. He hesitated before adding, "There was nothing to be gained on a political level from His Imperial Highness's death."

Tenuk started to say something snarky, but stopped himself. With the knight finally taking a step off his high horse, Tenuk didn't want to jinx it.

After a few minutes' walk, they came to an unmarked storefront. The building had no windows visible and had an air of being abandoned.

As Tenuk reached for the door latch, Sir Donaliel cleared his throat and said, "What exactly is this place?"

"Specialty food store," the inspector explained.

"It does not have a sign..." the knight pointed out.

"Doesn't need one. If you need to shop here, you know it's here," Tenuk explained before pushing the door open.

"Who needs to shop here?" Sir Donaliel whispered.

"Demons," Tenuk answered with a toothy grin before stepping inside.

The inside of the shop was dimly lit and crowded. Shelves filled with jars and vials crowded close together, narrow aisles left between them. A display case at the front of the store held an arrangement of unusual looking meats. Tenuk knew from experience that magic kept the contents preserved. Across the ceiling, thick ropes of webbing stretched through the rafters. In one corner of the web a giant spider clung to the ceiling. Its body was six feet long and its legs spread out a good ten feet around it. Bristly white hairs stuck out across its black chitinous body.

A noise issued from the spider, barely audible sounds that caused the already dim light in the shop to momentarily dim even further. A moment later a fluid wave poured up over one of the counters, a writhing mass of spiderlings clambering over one another on top of the wooden surface.

"Good morning, Inspector," the shrill voices of the spiderlings said in unison.

"Hey kids," Tenuk said matter-of-factly. "Got some questions for your grandpa if he's got some time."

The spider issued its fell noise again, and the spiderlings translated, "Grandpa says he has time."

"We're looking for someone who may have purchased a fellblade dagger recently," Tenuk asked.

The spider paused for a minute, shifting slightly in its web. Tenuk narrowed his eyes suspiciously. The spider didn't usually hesitate. Somehow Tenuk felt like the spider had finally noticed the knight standing closer to the door.

Finally, it spoke again and the children translated, "Grandpa didn't sell her anything."

"Her? Who is this 'her?'" Tenuk asked. "I think I missed something from the point where I brought up the fellblade."

"Grandpa doesn't know who she was," came the translation. "He thinks she came here knowing that demons came here, but he didn't help her."

Tenuk followed up with, "What did she look like?"

"Human," was the consensus answer from the spiderling swarm.

The inspector fought off the urge to point out that that wasn't very helpful, but he'd long since realized that not all races really perceived things like hair color and skin tone. Hell, Tenuk sometimes got them mixed up if they had similar coloration.

"Okay, fine," Tenuk sighed. "Assuming she found someone more talkative, who would they have sent her to?"

"The Sliding Baroness," the spiderlings translated.

"The sliding which?" Tenuk asked, his scaly face screwed up in confusion.

"I know who she is," Sir Donaliel quietly, startling the inspector. Tenuk had half forgotten the fae knight was there. As he looked back he noticed the fae seemed to almost glow in the dim light. Weird.

"Then I guess that's where we're going to next," Tenuk said. To the spider he said, "Thanks for your time. Oh, hey... before I leave, can I get a couple pints of that blue stuff?"

♦

Sir Donaliel felt vaguely ill as they approached the house, once elegant but fallen into disrepair. Its tottering gambrel roof rose menacingly above the hoary willows that surrounded it. The closer he got, the more uncomfortable he felt. It was as though a fly was buzzing just outside his peripheral vision, constantly irritating but never visible, or he had a phantom itch on a severed limb he never had.

On the way to the house he had noticed someone following them. It was either one person capable of illusory disguises or several people working in shifts. As the taint of the house started to affect the knight, he had more trouble keeping track of the people following them.

"You are not going to bring that in with you, are you?" the knight asked testily, his gaze indicating the jar of blue slime that Tenuk had purchased. It was a convenient distraction from the gnawing at his attention.

"Well, I haven't had a chance to drop it off at home," the inspector said with a shrug.

"Do you always bring your groceries with you while you are working?" Sir Donaliel snarked, the energy of the building making him testy.

"I wouldn't say always," Tenuk answered with a dismissive shrug. "But sometimes I don't have time to do much shopping with the hours I work. You gonna knock?"

Sir Donaliel realized with a jolt that he already stood at the door. Hoping that he had maintained his usual reserved expression, he reached up and rapped the knocker. A moment later an ashen-skinned servant opened the door and looked blankly at them without speaking.

"We are here to see the Sliding Baroness," the knight explained to the servant.

The servant stared at them a moment longer before turning on his heel and walking into the house. Sir Donaliel eventually assumed that the servant intended the open door to serve as an invitation. The knight ducked his head and entered. He heard Tenuk follow close behind.

The path they took lead them deeper into the house, through musty halls hung with paintings of alien vistas and lined with weapons and armor meant for inhuman entities.

A few moments later the servant opened a door that lead into a study, a roaring fire burning in the hearth. A padded, high-backed chair faced the fireplace, the contents of the chair not visible from the doorway. The servant stood dutifully by the door. Sir Donaliel strode forward and stopped just inside the room; the inspector followed him in and stood at his side. The door clicked shut behind them.

"Think I should have closed the front door?" Tenuk whispered.

Sir Donaliel shot the inspector a dirty look and then turned his attention back to the room, calling out, "Hello?"

"Please, come closer," came a hoarse voice from the chair.

The two of them walked towards the chair, circling it at a distance until they could see the occupant. The closer the fae came to the chair, the more the irritation grew, feeling like a hot iron tickling at the back of his eyes. The Sliding Baroness was slender and wore a loose robe that still clung close enough to her to highlight her slight feminine curves. One might have thought her figure shapely if not for the occasional writhing movement under the robe, as though rats crawled along her skin. A white porcelain mask covered her face, painted to suggest an elegant and mature woman. No details were visible beyond the token holes for eyes, nostrils, and mouth. Framing the mask, her hair was rich and lustrous, a curly cascade of blonde, purple and blue that rolled down her shoulders. Between her hairline and mask, a thin fleshy tendril occasionally writhed into sight, as though it was probing the air.

"Sir Donaliel," she croaked. "It is an honor to be visited by one of His Imperial Majesty's own knights. And who is this handsome fellow with you with, might I add, excellent taste in food?"

"This is Inspector Tenuk, of the City Watch," the knight introduced. "Inspector, may I present to you the Sliding Baroness."

"A pleasure," mumbled Tenuk.

"And to what do I owe this honor?" she asked. She sounded amused, but the fae could never be certain with that mask.

"We are investigating the murder of Prince Aleatoire. It is our understanding that you are the sort of person who might sell a fellblade," Sir Donaliel stated simply, letting the sentence rest between them a few moments.

Finally, the Sliding Baroness responded, "It seems an awful shame. You finally crawl your way out of the shadow of one dishonor, and yet here you are dealing with the Prince's problems again."

"Fellblade," Sir Donaliel snapped. "Do you possess one?"

"I do own a few. Well, one less than I did before. Sadly, one was recently stolen."

"Why do you have such things?" the knight asked, disgust compounding his annoyance and discomfort.

"I am a collector," she said. "I assure you all of my artifacts are registered as necessary."

"There are many things to collect," Sir Donaliel pointed out. "Why those?"

"A fellblade is almost impossible to destroy. They have to go somewhere," the Sliding Baroness answered. The fae could not tell if she shrugged or if that was some effect of whatever moved under her robes. "Would you rather some sinister cult had a secret stash of them?"

Shifting things back on topic, the knight asked, "You say one was stolen?"

"Yes," she said. "I filed the report yesterday."

Sir Donaliel shot a look at the inspector, who shrugged and commented, "She could have. I had constables check those earlier, but if she just submitted it yesterday it could still be in process."

"Convenient," the knight sneered.

"Bureaucracy," Tenuk said with a second shrug, as though the single word said it all.

"Why did you not call for the City Watch?" Sir Donaliel pressed.

"I was in no hurry," she said. "I knew who stole it and wrote all the pertinent details in my report."

"You know who stole it?" the knight asked, shock creeping into his voice.

"Yes," the Sliding Baroness responded.

When she didn't add any further details, Sir Donaliel impatiently asked, "Who was it?"

"Oh, a sweet young girl," she answered with a sigh. "Had quite the sob story. Wanted to buy the dagger from me."

"Do you know her name?" the knight queried impatiently.

"Yes, I can even tell you where she lives."

"And why did you not sell it to her?"

"I knew what she wanted to do with it," she said. Sir Donaliel was more certain that she shrugged on this occasion, but not entirely. "And to sell it to her, especially without the proper paperwork, would make me an accomplice to a crime. Even we demons find value in the Imperial Amnesty, and I am loathe to endanger my citizenship here."

"How did she steal it from you?" Sir Donaliel sighed. He wanted to be done with this. He wanted to be out of this house. His stomach roiled as though fire ants were brawling within it.

"While I am not a criminal investigator, I believe she 'ransacked' the sitting room where it was on display," she said.

"And you did not have any wards to stop her?" he said incredulously, the itch of dark magic nagging at him.

"I did, but they are not as good as they once were," she noted wistfully. "They say that that which is deathless cannot truly die, but they never say much about your joints or your memory. After all these countless eons, I'm just not as good at what I do anymore."

"Fine," the knight stiffly commented. "Did she say why she wanted to kill Prince Aleatoire?"

"Yes, but I will leave it to her to explain herself," the Sliding Baroness said coolly. Sir Donaliel began to feel that the painted smile on the mask was mocking him. "When you see her, all will become clear."

♦

As darkness fell, Tenuk grew nervous. Goblin Town was a dodgy place to go after the sun went down, especially if you were a constable. If the usual band of criminals wasn't enough, the assorted nocturnal predators (licensed and otherwise) gave the Inspector cause for concern. And then there was the matter of whoever followed them. Tenuk was sure Sir Donaliel had noticed. The fae had lost some of his game face while dealing with the home of the Sliding Baroness and it was clear he was tracking the same pursuers that Tenuk had noticed. He couldn't decide how he felt about the knight's faint luminescence as they traveled through a bad part of town. Part of him wanted to take a few steps back to make the fae the more obvious target.

They had an escort of a half-dozen patrol officers from the constabulary. Hopefully that would be enough if things went pear-shaped. Tenuk didn't expect their person of interest to be that much trouble, but she was the least of the threats the constables faced here.

The boarding house they were headed to was deep in the heart of the neighborhood. One of several seedy little dives where those with little resources could hide from the elements. It usually wasn't worth it to the constables to raid places like this.

"So I gotta ask," Tenuk finally said as they walked through the twilight. "My curiosity is just killing me. What was this dishonor the Sliding Baroness gave you crap about?"

Sir Donaliel did not respond.

"Oh, c'mon," Tenuk said. "We're going into the shit part of town, after a woman who killed a nephilim prince with a fellblade. We could die. Don't tell me you are going to hold out on telling me something that even demons know about."

With some hesitation the knight replied, "I will not go into details, but suffice to say that there is a distinction in the Imperial government between 'what is proper' and 'what you can accomplish.' This is a lesson I only learned the difficult way. This occurred when my investigation of a threat to the Imperial Crown put me at odds with higher ranking ministers. They did not dare strip me of my knighthood, so they instead chose to assign me the ignoble duty of defending Prince Aleatoire. With several years of hard work, I was able to be reassigned to a marginally better duty. Prince Aleatoire's demise has brought me back to cleaning up after His Imperial Highness once again."

Tenuk opened his mouth to reply, closed it, then opened it again and paused. Finally he just said, "Well, crap."

Ten silent minutes later, they arrived at their destination. Tenuk took the lead when they got to the building, stepping up to knock on the front door. A few moments later the door opened and the inspector looked down to see a wizened gnome looking suspiciously up at the drakin. Behind the gnome Tenuk saw a dozen or so of the gnome's progeny, with his wife unabashedly nursing the latest addition as she stood watching from the hallway. The sulfurous smell of cabbage rolled out the door.

The gnome didn't say a thing, so Tenuk stated, "We're here for Lady Elizabeth."

"I think you've got the wrong end of town if you're looking for a noblewoman, constable," the gnome said with a sly grin on his face.

"Don't get cute, stumpy," Tenuk spat back. "You can either be helpful or we can see if this building is as flammable as it looks." He exhaled slowly and a tongue of flame danced briefly around his lips.

"Ah, yes, you must mean the human," the gnome said. His skin was a little more pale, but he didn't drop the smug grin. "I don't ask names. Bad for business. You'll find her at the top of the stairs on the right."

Tenuk signaled to the other constables to take up position outside while he and Sir Donaliel went in. Wading through the gnomish children staring curiously at them, the constable and the knight made their way up the stairs.

At the relevant door, the two looked at one another, the knight finally reaching up to knock on the door as he called out, "Lady Elizabeth?"

"Come in," replied a woman's voice from within. The knight pushed open the door and walked into the room, Tenuk following close behind.

Lady Elizabeth sat facing away from the door in the room's only chair. She seemed to be looking out a window that faced onto an alley. The only other furniture was a crudely made bed and small table holding a washbasin. From behind she was dark haired and slim, but as she slowly pushed herself to her feet and turned to face them they saw that a belly swollen with child interrupted her slight build.

"Crap," muttered Tenuk.

"Lady Elizabeth," the knight said. "I am Sir Donaliel of the Sun Guard; this is Inspector Tenuk of the City Watch." Tenuk raised a taloned hand in greeting. "We're here to ask you some questions about the death of Prince Aleatoire."

"I was wondering how long it would be before someone showed up," she said with a sad tone in her voice. She looked young, probably no more than seventeen. But stress and malnutrition, combined with whatever problems she may have had with pregnancy, leant her features a more mature caste.

"Did you murder Prince Aleatoire?" Sir Donaliel inquired bluntly.

After a moment of hesitation, she looked away and said softly, "Yes."

Sensing that the knight was about to say something further, Tenuk interrupted him by asking, "Why'd you do it?"

She placed her hands on her swollen belly and said, "Do you really need to ask?" After a moment she added, "I'd been slumming, going to revels, getting into trouble. My parents didn't believe me when I told them who the father was. They wanted me to drink the tea that would make this all go away, in hopes that I might still be marriageable. I refused, they disowned me. Al didn't care. He just laughed and told me he wasn't interested in me or the child. I was... I was hurt, and angry."

The knight was about to speak again when Tenuk interrupted again, "How did you get the money to go shopping for a fellblade?"

"I didn't, really," she said with a shrug. She continued to look away from them. "An uncle I only barely know took pity on me and sent me some money to live off of. Gave me an offer to pay for anything I needed and the addresses where I could purchase the tools for vengeance."

"The old spider and the Sliding Baroness both refused to sell you the fellblade," the inspector added for her. "You found the Baroness' dagger easy to steal, so you did."

The young noblewoman nodded numbly.

"How'd you get the jump on a nephilim?"

"He was high on something and was stumbling through the revel," she said, sobbing slightly as she did. "Between the drugs and the music, I doubt he even heard anything I said before I...I..." Tears and sobbing overwhelmed the rest of her words.

Tenuk hooked the knight by the elbow and led him back towards the door saying, "We'll be right back."

Once outside the room, with the door closed, Sir Donaliel whispered, "Why did you persist in interrupting me in there?"

"Because you were going to place her under arrest," Tenuk replied.

"That is what we are here to do."

"Don't you find it a little weird that a penniless pregnant noblewoman cast out of her family was able to get hold of a fellblade?" Tenuk asked. "They wanted Prince Al dead and they wanted us to know who did it."

"I do not see your point," Sir Donaliel said.

"We arrest her, she'll be executed for treason," the inspector shot back. "If Their Imperial Majesties are feeling generous, she'll be allowed to give birth to her child and then get executed. And in the end her crime was mainly trusting the wrong people and letting herself be a scapegoat."

"We cannot let people think they can attack the Imperial family without consequence," the knight emphasized.

"Then go after the people responsible," Tenuk responded. "Go after the uncle who put her up to this, work to find evidence of a conspiracy between the uncle and the Sliding Baroness. Really, are you looking for justice here or to get a pregnant girl killed because she crossed a prince that no one really liked?"

Sir Donaliel hesitated and looked away, the conflicting emotions evident on his face.

"You bust open a conspiracy to strike out at a low-hanging fruit of the Imperial family, it will be quite a feather in your cap," Tenuk wheedled.

"Or make things worse for myself," the knight countered. "The girl will direct investigation towards a conspiracy whether she is arrested or not."

"Maybe, maybe not," Tenuk said. "Do you trust Their Imperial Majesties to put the effort towards it? If we do this ourselves, we can make sure it goes the way we want it. Or do you want to just stick with what you can accomplish rather than what's 'proper.'"

"What about the girl?" Sir Donaliel asked, ignoring the jab. "What becomes of young Lady Elizabeth?"

"We stash her somewhere safe," Tenuk responded. "I've got some money tucked away to help keep her safe and get her a reasonable midwife. She can serve as a witness when you bring the other bastards down. If need-be I can probably get her set up in another city with another identity, and she can start her life fresh."

♦

They had spent perhaps ten minutes questioning the young woman about the details of her theft of the fellblade, the murder of Prince Aleatoire, and the role of her uncle when a knock came at the door. Tenuk and Sir Donaliel exchanged wary, questioning glances. Sir Donaliel hoped his look conveyed a question along the lines of, "Are you expecting someone?" and he suspected Tenuk's look asked the same.

As the knight drew his sword and turned to face the door, Lady Elizabeth whispered hysterically, "What's going on?" The fae glanced at Tenuk and saw that he similarly had drawn his long dagger and faced the door.

"Come in," Sir Donaliel offered.

An old woman shuffled in through the door, grey-haired and dressed in filthy rags. Sir Donaliel recognized her as one of the faces he had seen following them through the streets. She looked coyly at the knight and the inspector as she raised her gnarled hands in innocence.

"Drop the disguise," Sir Donaliel commanded.

The woman cackled in a shrill voice. Within a few seconds her voice had deepened and gained a musical quality to it. The image of the crone shriveled away like paper in a fire, revealing a dark haired youth with white wings blossoming from his back. The boy continued to hold his hands, now small and perfect and pink, in a gesture of helplessness. Lady Elizabeth gasped from the back of the room.

"Your Highness," Sir Donaliel said, his mind reeling from the surprise.

"You must be Prince Gabriel," Tenuk remarked drily. "Head of Her Imperial Majesty's Moon Watch. Hey, Sir Donaliel, I know there's a certain amount of, whaddya call it, animosity when other agencies step in on the Sun Guard—"

"What are you doing here?" the knight interrupted, uninterested in the drakin's jibes.

"Making sure you arrest the murderer and the investigation gets wrapped up as it should," the prince replied.

"What do you mean?" Sir Donaliel asked.

Tenuk shook his head, "Oh, this is rich."

"What do you mean?!" the fae repeated, emotion creeping into his normally gentle voice.

"Does your mommy know you killed your little brother?" Tenuk sneered.

"The order comes from the highest levels," the nephilim responded. With a shrug he added, "Which also explains some of the gaps in the arrangements. Had I arranged this, I assure you I would not be here to make sure it reached a satisfactory ending."

Comprehension dawned in the knight's mind and he asked, "Prince Aleatoire was too much of a liability, so you arranged to have him murdered?"

"The Imperial Crown commends you both on your fine work," Prince Gabriel said. "We will have you sign off your reports regarding this incident and you will both receive high accolades for accosting this murderer."

"If you think I'm going to be your trained monkey in this little farce," Tenuk replied, outraged, "you can just shove it in—"

Gabriel interrupted the drakin's tirade by executing a dancing lunge, gliding inside of the drakin's reach. Grabbing the inspector's wrist, the prince shifted his weight to throw Tenuk off balance. The pair spun like lovers towards Lady Elizabeth, Tenuk's long dagger nearly cutting her head off as his weight pushed the blade through her neck.

♦

Tenuk stared dumbly at the girl as her life faded from her eyes, his grip on his blade silently tightening.

"We are willing to take this to great lengths in order to ensure its satisfactory completion," Gabriel said. "Your reports will indicate that she struggled when you found her. She resisted arrest. You tried to take her in alive, but she was remarkably fierce. She was the sort of woman who could take out a scion of the Imperial Family, and proved to be quite a threat here. Please do not force me to add further casualties to this arrest gone wrong."

"That's it, asshole," Tenuk said through his clenched jaw as he turned to face the prince. His breathing grew heavy and smoke slowly billowed out in streams from his nostrils. "You're going down for this bullshit."

The drakin tried to lunge at the nephilim, but found thin but strong arms restraining him.

"Let it go, Tenuk," Sir Donaliel's voice said in the inspector's ear. "Believe my words when I tell you that you do not want to do this."

"Oh, I really want this," Tenuk replied as he thrashed to escape Sir Donaliel's grip. "I really fucking want this."

"You should listen to your friend, Inspector Tenuk," Gabriel counseled. "Or it could even be Lieutenant Inspector Tenuk. The Imperial Crown can give just as well as it can take away. When you've calmed down, you may want to consider that when you decide what to do next."

Tenuk's only response was a bellow of rage, flames rolling out from his wide-stretched mouth.

♦

Sir Donaliel and Tenuk sat slumped on the steps of the flophouse as the sun rose over the city. The knight's rigid posture had collapsed under the events of the day, while the inspector just looked tired. They'd sent their escort home hours before. The threat of Goblin Town no longer seemed as dire. All they seemed capable of was staring bleakly at the debris strewn streets.

"You ever have to deal with this level of bullshit?" Tenuk finally asked after a couple hours.

"Yes," Sir Donaliel admitted.

"Yeah, I guess you have. You going to take the deal?" the inspector asked.

"I do not see much alternative," Sir Donaliel replied. "I… have worked too long and hard to make more enemies. Are you going to take it, 'Lieutenant Inspector?'"

"You still want to protect these assholes?" Tenuk asked, avoiding the question.

Sir Donaliel in turn avoided the question and asked, "What is the next step?"

Tenuk did not reply right away. He just stared at the street. Finally, he answered, "I'm thinking food. I'm famished."

"Is that all you think about?" the knight asked, exasperated.

"Hey, the job's a lot harder to do on an empty stomach," the inspector said with forced humor as he stood from his seat on the steps. "We can't all get by on thimbles full of dandelion wine. C'mon. I'm thinking of going to Vinnie's. I'll buy ya a chutney."

"I have heard of this place," the knight replied as he slowly unfolded his long limbs to get to his feet. "Do people not die from the food there?"

"Sometimes, but I'm sure Vinnie will take your delicate constitution in mind and let you order off of the kids' menu," the inspector jibed.

Sir Donaliel sighed and followed Tenuk into the breaking dawn.

**Jeremy Zimmerman** is a county bureaucrat by day, but by night he turns to his writing as an outlet for the voices in his head. After writing for game companies, he has shifted his focus to fiction. His tales can be found in *Crossed Genres Magazine, Wily Writers Speculative Fiction, 10Flash Quarterly* and anthologies by Timid Pirate Publishing. Visit his website at http://www.bolthy.com for more info.

# "Puppet Play"

## by Kelli D. Meyer

Silence settled over the kitchen as the sound of the slap faded. It was like we were all frozen; nobody moved until Dad raised his arm. Then Mom took a few steps back and put her arms up to protect herself, guarding her face. But he didn't make a move toward her; he just smoothed his hand over his own face where Mom's palm print was standing out in red. While he was standing like that, looking stunned, Mom's left arm shot out, and she grabbed her steaming cup of tea off the counter. With a look of horror, she threw her tea at his face. Dad saw it coming and turned away, so most of the hot liquid hit the side of his head and his shoulder, but it still must have hurt. At least he sounded like it hurt when he started cussing.

Good. It was about time. He had it coming.

But I do feel kind of bad. He got really mad at her. I think he might have hit her if he hadn't been so late for work. At least he might have tried, but I wouldn't have let him.

Still, he deserved it, so I don't feel *that* bad. And seeing his face was worth it. He was speechless that sweet little Mom would do something like that just because he said she was stupid. Again.

Not that she *really* did it. Her face was even more shocked than his. And she did try to fight me. But I'm stronger than they are. I didn't even have to move my own arms to make it happen. Not like I used to.

The first time I did it was last summer, before I started eleventh grade, and it was an accident. I still don't really know what happened.

It was an oven-hot, dry day, so hot it was hard to breathe, so we all had our shirts off. At least the sweat had a chance to evaporate instead of just making my shirt soggy. I was playing ball with the guys, and Jimmy—the Jimidiot—sucked, as usual. He had landed on my team, and we stuck him in right field where he'd be out of the way. Plus that way we didn't have to look too much at his fish-belly white man-boobs. That boy could totally wear a bra.

We'd managed to play eight and a half innings without hardly thinking about Jimmy at all, but then wouldn't you know it, the very last batter hit a fly ball right at him with two on base. If he caught it, we'd win, but what were the chances of that? I was watching that ball come straight down over Jimmy's head, and he was just standing there, lips moving like he was singing to himself.

"Dammit, Jimmy, the ball!" I hollered. And everyone around me was hollering, too. Calls of "Jimidiot, look!" and "Catch it!" and "You stupid..." all ran together, but Jimmy didn't act like he heard any of us. He just kept singing to himself.

I was concentrating so hard on Jimmy that I hardly noticed when my arm shot up, all by itself without my thinking about it, like I could help him catch the ball. But then all of a sudden Jimmy's arm shot up, too. He jerked like he'd been goosed and looked at his arm like it was possessed, like it wasn't even part of him. I saw his eyes get wide all the way across the field. He didn't even watch the ball, just his arm. When the ball fell right into his glove, he didn't seem to notice, but I closed my hand to hold it, and Jimmy's glove closed, too. I'll be damned if we didn't win the game, and Jimmy was a hero. Some of the guys even picked him up—man-boobs and all—and carried him around on their shoulders.

Afterwards, while we were having Cokes at Sonic— we sprang for Jimmy's, and I thought he was going to bust he was so happy—he kept rubbing and flexing his hand, shaking it and smacking it against the table and looking at it like it might attack him.

At one point he leaned over and loud-whispered into my ear, "Mikey, did you see what my hand did?"

"Yeah, Jimmy, I saw. You caught the ball."

"Uh, uh, Mikey. Uh uh. My hand did it." He shoved his hand in my face, dirty fingers almost touching my nose.

"Right. You caught the ball with your hand. You did good, Jimid... Jimmy."

I thought he'd grin. He has this big, lopsided grin that makes him look about three years old. But he didn't crack a smile at all. Instead, he just looked confused. Not that that's an unusual look for him.

"My *hand* did it," he repeated, totally serious, this time holding the hand in question in front of his own face and looking at each finger one by one.

"OK, right, your hand did it."

He stopped looking at his hand and looked at me, nodding solemnly, eyes big like I'd just said something incredibly profound.

Actually, I wasn't real sure what had happened, but I *was* sure I wanted to find out if I could make it happen again. If I could, this held real humor potential.

It didn't take long for the perfect opportunity to present itself. Jimmy had his giant-sized drink in his hand, one of those disgusting cherry things he likes, so I just concentrated like crazy on his hand and then clenched my fist—hard. For a split second I didn't think anything was going to happen, then Jimmy's eyebrows shot up, and that drink exploded like a grenade. Syrupy cherry Coke splattered all over Jimmy, and Adam, Mark, and Eric suffered collateral damage. Eric even had Styrofoam shrapnel in his hair.

I was far enough away to escape with just a few splashes, but I was laughing so hard I didn't even care. Eric cared. He climbed over the table like he was going to tear Jimmy's head off, but Adam grabbed his shirt and reeled him in. Pretty soon we were all laughing, except for Jimmy. He was staring at his hand again, and he looked kinda scared. The rest of us were cracking up so loud the Sonic lady came out and told us to settle down or vacate the premises, which just made us laugh harder. Being run away from Sonic!

The rest of the summer, while Eric was trying out his new whiskers with a sickly looking moustache and Mark was ruining his dad's clutch learning to drive a stick shift and Adam was spending all his time with Caroline trying to get to second base, I was learning how to control puppets. People, I mean. Turns out that if I can see them, I can control them. At least, I can control their bodies.

I tried it with a couple of other people just to make sure my power extended beyond Jimmy, but mostly I kept using Jimmy as my test case. He's a nice enough guy, but he's always been a little odd—what with all the singing to himself and counting his French fries and wearing that coach's whistle around his neck all the time. I figured he'd be the least likely to catch on to the fact that somebody else was pulling the strings, or be believed if he did figure it out. I mean, life is weird enough when you're Jimmy, so what's a little more weirdness?

After just a few more tries, I discovered that I could move him without moving myself. That really opened up my options. I mean, what's the point of making people do stupid things if *you* have to do them, too? By the time school started, I'd made Jimmy moon Jennifer Miller, stick a French fry—number forty-seven—up his nose, and flip off Chuck Handel, a varsity linebacker. That last one was a double-whammy on poor Jimmy because right after I stopped making him move, Chuck took over and turned him into a projectile. Luckily Jimmy is pretty well-padded, so he just ended up with some bruises and scrapes. Well, that and he got a little twitchy, even weirder than he used to be. Instead of singing all the time, he started talking to his hands. Eric said later that he'd heard Jimmy saying over and over, "hands behave, hands behave, hands behave," like he was praying or something. He said it was totally hilarious.

Next time I saw him, Jimmy was doing the same thing, and Eric was with me. While we watched, Mrs. Applebee, the walrus-looking substitute teacher, walked by in her sausage-tight polyester pants. I couldn't resist. Jimmy was just chanting as he walked along, "hands behave, hands behave," when one of those hands jerked out and grabbed a big old fistful of Applebee ass. I don't know which one of them squealed louder. Eric and I laughed so hard we just about pissed our pants. Eric didn't know I'd done it, which was a shame, but it was still damn funny.

That afternoon, wouldn't you know it, Mrs. Applebee was subbing for my algebra class. Sometimes things just come together, you know? When she went to write her name on the board—like there's anyone in school who *doesn't* know who she is—the chalk squeaked through "Mrs. Applebee," then kept right on going through "loves Jimmy Martin," and finished with a big old heart. You could have heard a pin drop. Right up until she started screeching, and that set all the kids off. We were all laughing and making kissing noises, and a couple of the girls started singing, "Applebee and Jimmy sitting in a tree..." It was awesome.

The rest of this year has been a blast. My school has won every game I've gone to because the opposing teams just keep dropping balls or getting injured, and I've had hardly any homework since the teachers just don't seem to be able to get the words out to assign any.

And then there was Jenny.

After Jimmy mooned her, I jumped on the opportunity to comfort her and tell her what a jerk I thought he'd been. She ate it up so much that when I asked her to go see a movie with me she said yes. And after the movie, she just kept saying yes. Learning to control vocal cords has been one of my greatest achievements; they're a lot harder than hands. And Jenny's hands cooperated just fine. She unbuttoned her shirt and pulled down her jeans like it was her idea. But I couldn't quite get her eyes to look right, and seeing her look scared was ruining the mood, so I finally just closed her eyes. Everything went great after that. And it's not like I really hurt her or anything; everyone says she puts out anyway. Still, it's too bad that Jenny's acted weird around me since that night, except when I make her act nice, of course.

So that's been my year, a real blast… until this afternoon. I'd been psyched because of Mom slapping Dad, and then I'd topped off my morning with a little humor following the slapping theme: Jimmy was hilarious when he stood up in front of the class during English and hit himself in the face a few times. I let him stop when he started crying, though, because the laughter was starting to fade.

Then in fifth period algebra, I kept hearing people whispering Jimmy's name. I thought it was because of what I'd done that morning, and I was pretty pumped. If only I could tell somebody it was really me who did it.

But then Adam leaned over and told me what they were really saying.

"Dude, can you believe what the Jimidiot did?"

"Heh heh, yeah, I was there."

"Huh? You were in gym with me last period."

"Last period? What are you talking about?"

"I'm talking about wood shop, last period, the Jimidiot. Can you believe it? He's really gone around the bend this time."

"Wood shop?" I hadn't been near the wood shop, and I could only control people when I could see them, so whatever Jimmy had done, he'd done it without any help from me.

Adam continued: "Yeah, I heard he was doing that crazy, "hands behave" chant the whole time he was doing it. Didn't scream or anything."

"Doing what? What did he do?" My stomach felt small and hard as a baseball.

"Dude, he cut off his hand. With some nasty saw thing they have in there. Tony Henson said he was sitting all the way on the other side of the room, and he showed me the blood he got on his shirt. That shit was spraying *everywhere*."

"His hand? He cut it *off*?"

"Yeah, isn't that wild? The nurse came, but she wouldn't touch the thing. Coach Hillerman had to pick it up and put it in ice. They sent it to the hospital with Jimmy. Like maybe they'll just sew it back on or something. Wouldn't that be cool?"

I thought I might throw up. My mouth was too wet; I had to keep swallowing spit to keep from drooling, and I felt little beads of sweat emerge on my temples. But I said, "Cool. Yeah, that would be cool." Then I stood up and walked out of the classroom.

I got out to my car before I figured out what I was doing. I needed to go home. I needed to tell Mom I was sorry, explain to her what had happened. I needed her to help me fix it. But I was shaking too hard to drive. Funny, I could control everyone else's bodies, but I couldn't control my own. I had to settle for calling her. She picked up on the second ring.

"Michael? What's wrong?" Mom's not psychic, she just has caller ID, and I never call her during the day, so there being something wrong was a pretty safe guess.

"Mom? Something happened."

"Sweetie, are you okay? Who...? Hold on, I think your dad just came in. Honey?"

Mom must have set the phone down then, but I could hear everything that happened.

"Bob, what are you doing home?"

"I've been thinking about this morning, about what you did." Even muffled the way it was, I could recognize Dad's "mean" voice.

"Mom!" But she didn't hear me.

"Honey, I..."

"Don't honey me, you stupid bitch."

I heard a crash then, and Mom screamed. I hollered into the phone, "Dad! No! It was me!" But nobody paid any attention. All I could hear was hitting, the sound of fists on flesh, and Mom whimpering. But I couldn't see them, so I couldn't make Mom fight back, and I couldn't make Dad stop.

After awhile, when I didn't hear anything anymore, I clicked the "end" button on my phone. I leaned my head back against the headrest and breathed hard for a minute. Then I sat up and started the car. I'd been wrong. It wasn't Mom I needed to see. I needed to see Dad.

◆◆◆

**Kelli D. Meyer** is a graduate of the Odyssey Fantasy Writing Workshop and has won numerous awards for her writing, including multiple honorable mentions in the international *Writers of the Future Contest*. Her fiction has been published most recently by *OnThePremises.com, WilyWriters.com*, and *FlashMe.com*. One of her stories/screenplays has been produced as a film, titled "Spoiled Rotten", which won the Platinum Award in its category at the Houston International Film Festival and was chosen for the Dragon*Con Film Festival.

She lives outside of Houston with her husband, three dogs, two horses, and way too many cats.

Her website is www.kellidmeyer.com.

# ABOUT WILY WRITERS

Wily Writers was born on October 31st, 2008, when the private writers group was formed by Angel Leigh McCoy and Ripley Patton. On Valentine's Day, 2009, we launched (with great joy) the Wily Writers Speculative Fiction site where all the stories in this book appeared as an audio podcast.

Wily Writers is a labor of love dedicated to helping writers build their careers, and it continues to be an amazing and fulfilling adventure. We have attracted wondrous talent to the site and have also had to reject many incredible stories. The friends of Wily Writers continue to multiply. We're blessed to have met so many great people.

Visit WilyWriters.com to find the stories in this book as audio podcasts. Drop us a line, and let us know what you think at wily@nwlink.com, or join us at Goodreads for a discussion!

# ABOUT THE EDITOR

Angel Leigh McCoy is an award-winning writer herself. She has worked for game companies for many years and is currently writing dialogue for a highly anticipated computer game, *Guild Wars 2,* at ArenaNet. Horror and dark fantasy are her genres for fiction. She has published short stories in numerous anthologies and magazines.

Visit her at AngelMcCoy.com.